Caitlin King can't believe that her shopaholic cousin actually bought two ghosts off of eBay. But she can't ignore the truth when she starts seeing sexy Liam O'Reilly, who's been dead for over a hundred years. He's a fascinating specter, and the more time Caitlin spends with him, the closer they become—sending them both spiraling into a star-crossed tailspin. No matter how desperately they long for each other, there's just no future with a guy who's already stopped breathing.

In order to help Liam and his twin sister, Anna, leave their earthly limbo and cross over into the light, Caitlin must find the ghost of Anna's fiancé. But a malevolent spirit is dead set against Anna moving on. Now Caitlin will have to unravel the mystery surrounding the twins' past lives in order to keep Liam's spirit safe—even if it means sacrificing her heart in the process.

Visit us at www.kensingtonbooks.com

I0677566

Books by Sandra Cox

Mutants Series
Love, Lattes and Mutants
Love, Lattes and Danger

Ghost for Sale

Published by Kensington Publishing Corporation

Ghost For Sale

Sandra Cox

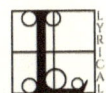

LYRICAL PRESS
Kensington Publishing Corp.
www.kensingtonbooks.com

First Electronic Edition: September 2015
eISBN-13: 978-1-61650-773-2
eISBN-10: 1-61650-773-X

First Print Edition: September 2015
ISBN-13: 978-1-61650-774-9
ISBN-10: 1-61650-774-8

Printed in the United States of America

For Mike, who always supports my literary efforts,
And Camille, whose mission has been to fatten me up and change my
politics

Acknowledgements

As always, thanks to my editor Paige Christian

Renee Rocco, Managing Director

And to my agent Joyce Holland

Chapter 1

Brring. The shriek of the doorbell caused me to jump, interrupting my first morning jolt of caffeine, as hot liquid sloshed over the sides and burned me. "Crap." I thumped the cup down and trotted to the door, shaking my stinging fingers.

My irritation faded when I opened the door.

A young delivery man dressed in standard tan gave me an appreciative once over. I returned the favor. "Miss VanLier?" He held a box in one hand and a clipboard and pen in the other. Lust turned my brain to mush. I reached for the clipboard and scratched my name.

"Miss King?"

"Yes."

"I'm sorry. But I need Miss VanLier's signature."

"Oops. Wait right there." I held up a finger and walked backward till I was out of sight, then sprinted for my cousin's bedroom. "HDM at the door, Marcy."

"Hot delivery man?" She sat up.

"Yup. A Mr. Hottie."

"What's he want?"

"He's got a box that I can't sign for. Did you order those red stilettoes?"

She looked at me and mumbled, "They didn't have them in my size." Her eyes widened. "My ghosts!"

"What?"

"My ghosts. I bought two on eBay." She jumped out of bed.

"What?"

"Caitlin, you're repeating yourself. I bought two ghosts on eBay."

"No. Really? How much?"

"Three thousand apiece." She reached for the robe at the foot of her bed and threw it on.

Pressure began to build at my temples. "Why would you spend six thousand dollars for ghosts?"

"Why not?" She trotted out of the room and raced down the hall.

Good question. Marcy's parents were richer than God. Spending a few thou on a whim was no big deal. My parents weren't exactly poor, but their fortunes paled in comparison to my mom's sister's family.

I hauled butt after her. "You don't really believe that stuff, do you?"

"Why else would I have bought them?"

Why indeed?

We made it to the door in a dead heat.

"Are you Miss VanLier?" HDM asked.

"Yes, that's right." She reached for the pen and clipboard. His glassy gaze traveled back and forth between the two of us, lingering on my short-shorts.

"She inherited those legs from her momma. At least that's what Aunt always tells us," Marcy put in helpfully as she intercepted the look.

Mr. HDM reddened, thrust the package at her, and beat a retreat.

She studied the return address. "It's my ghosts. But the package is ripped."

"I'll say." The box was busted, split at the seams. "We should have been paying more attention to the package and less to the delivery boy."

"It doesn't matter. I can't wait to see my specters." She clutched it to her breasts like a long lost child and headed to the kitchen, leaving me to shut the door. I watched the HDM drive away, then trotted after her.

"You opened it," I said, disappointed I'd missed the reveal.

"No, the tube was cracked and the cork out. My ghost escaped somewhere between here and Florida." She rubbed her forehead as if warding off a headache.

A chill swept down my spine. Then sanity returned. Ghost indeed.

"Jonas Bromwell is going to reimburse me for this purchase. I'm not paying three thousand for a cracked test tube. My daddy taught me the value of a dollar." Hands splayed on her waist, she glared at the broken cylinder.

"Yeah, and I wonder if your idea of value is going to equal his."

"Say what?"

"Nothing. What about the other one?" I pointed at the still intact tube. Her face brightened. She looked at me, grinned, and picked it up with perfectly manicured nails.

Slowly, she pulled out the cork, drawing out the moment, then *pop*. "Welcome to your new home, ghost."

A current of electricity traveled along my skin and trailed down my arms in a slow, sensuous slide. Heat escalated and my arms burned. "Ouch. Ouch. Ouch." As I flailed around, the smell of cinnamon and tart limes teased my senses. The hairs on my neck stood on end. Goose bumps roughened my skin. *What the...*

"Caitlin, what is wrong with you?"

"I have no idea," I wailed. "My arms feel on fire. Do you smell that?"

Marcy dutifully lifted her nose and sniffed. "Smell what? Your arms have just gone to sleep. That's happened to me before. Just keep shaking them and they'll feel better in no time."

Right. I ran to the sink, turned on the cold water, and stuck them under it. The heat disappeared as quickly as it had come. The smell was gone too. *This is weird.* I touched my arms, for any lingering warmth, but they were cool from the water. My skin looked perfectly normal, no blisters.

"Are you better?"

"Yes."

"I would have never thought about running water for a muscle cramp. I'll remember that next time."

I opened my mouth to correct her, then promptly shut it. What was the point?

Marcy's attention turned back to the test tube. She waited expectantly, her eyes wide. As the minutes ticked away, the look of expectation turned to disappointment. "That thief, I'm going to ask for all my money back. He sold me empty test tubes."

I tried to work up a "well duh." But I couldn't quite do it, maybe because I was shaking like a leaf.

When I didn't respond, my cousin looked at me. The frown on her lovely features deepened. "What's wrong with you? You're white as a sheet and trembling."

Not for a million bucks or a thousand pair of shoes would I admit I might have just experienced my first ghostly encounter. I croaked the first thing that came to mind. "Sugar."

She pulled out a box of donuts, tossed them on the table, just missing an empty juice glass, and I fell into the chair.

"Want a Pepsi?"

"Please."

"I can't believe I got scammed. I was so sure I was buying ghosts. The seller seemed so sincere." She pulled a can out of the fridge and handed it to me. I drank it so fast I choked, and she slapped me on the back.

"I'm fine." I waved her away.

"Here, have a donut."

I reached for a glazed, inhaling the yeasty confection before brushing my palms together to get the sticky icing off my fingers.

"There, you're looking better." She beamed, then turned and walked out.

I loved my cousin, and her abrupt mood changes were just part of her charm, but this one left me a bit off balance. Clearly, she was already over her ghost disappointment and had moved on to her next obsession.

As soon as she left, I slipped out of the room and went to the little study off my bedroom, opened my laptop, and googled paranormal activity. In moments, I was immersed. Time disappeared as I tried to find a rational explanation for the strange scent that had appeared when the top popped on the tube, along with the kilowatt voltage that had fried my skin without leaving a mark.

"I'm leaving now." Marcy spoke from the doorway.

My breath caught and I clutched my heart. "You scared me. What time is it?" I looked at the tick-tock cat clock on my wall, disoriented. "Six o'clock," we said in unison, me in disbelief.

"Have you been networking all this time?"

"Yeah." I took the coward's way out and didn't try to explain I'd been researching paranormal activity—ghosts in particular—not chatting socially. I'd be totally humiliated if my sophisticated cousin thought I was a geek. "You look great, Marcy." She wore faded jean capris and a crimson silk shirt over a red halter, topped off with chunky red jewelry. "I didn't think the party was till later."

"Cookout on the patio."

"Gotcha. Have fun."

"Sure you don't want to go?" A set of bangle bracelets jingled on her arm as she shifted her little red clutch to her other hand.

For a moment, I considered it. But I had a headache I couldn't shake, and the nerves under my skin were twitching. "I'll catch the next one."

"All right. Feel better." She gave me an airy wave of her fingers before she strolled out of the room.

"Have fun," I called after her, then winced as it notched up my headache. I shut my laptop and stretched. Maybe a swim would clear my head. I put on my black one-piece and headed for the pool, my cork thongs clopping against the warm cement. The glistening liquid beckoned. After toeing off my footwear, I dove in.

The cold splash of water shocked me and cleared my head. I floated on my back, buoyant, mindless. The sun still had an hour before it would set, but already the sky had turned a lovely shade of red. My body went limp and my headache disappeared.

Interspersed with the smell of chlorine, a light scent drifted toward me. For a moment, I enjoyed the sensual masculine fragrance. The next instant my body went rigid. *Cinnamon and tart limes!* Stiff as a board, I lost my buoyancy and went under. I kicked to the surface, coughing and choking. As I dog-paddled and pushed my streaming hair out of my face, a shadow fell across the pool.

My heart gave a hard thump. "Who's there?" I scrubbed droplets out of my eyes but couldn't see anything.

The sky clouded and turned overcast as the wind cooled and picked up, causing the water to ripple. Goose bumps rose on my arms and legs that had nothing to do with the weather. The shadow swayed back and forth in rhythm with the wind, beginning to take shape.

My insides turned to ice, my breath coming in short, sharp pants.

The next moment, a shimmery silhouette of a man lay across the water.

With more speed than grace, I sprinted for the opposite side of the pool. Water churned as I kicked out. As soon as I reached the ladder, I grasped it and whipped around. "Who's there?" I squeaked again. Only silence. The shadow, or whatever, was gone. The only scent the evening breeze carried was chlorine.

My muscles bunched and jumped as I pulled myself out of the pool. Pressure building in my head, I grabbed a thick white towel, wrapped it around me, and raced into the bungalow just as the phone rang. My feet wet, I slipped and slid across the tile floor as I hurried to answer it. "Hello?"

"Caitlin, how are you?" Laughing voices and music sounded in the background.

"Clayton?" Surprise jolted me.

"Yeah, I'm back. I was going to surprise you. Thought you'd be at Richie's. Want me to come over?"

"I'd love for you to," I responded with more enthusiasm than poor Clayton usually received from me.

"I'm on my way." He clicked off.

"Hurry," I muttered to the silent phone.

I looked furtively around as I raced to the bedroom to change clothes. I didn't know what I was worrying about. We had an excellent alarm system. Nonetheless, I locked myself in the bedroom and dressed in record time. I peeked out the door. Reassured no one was there, I skulked into the hallway and waited for Clayton. When the buzzer sounded, I opened the door and threw myself into his arms.

His eyebrows rose, his body went rigid, and his face registered stunned surprise...for about five seconds. "This is more like it." He kissed me enthusiastically, his hands busy as little bees.

I drew back. "I'm sorry, Clayton. I didn't mean to give you the wrong impression." Clayton and I went out occasionally, but we weren't an item.

He took a deep inhale and got his breathing under control. His arms dropped from my shoulders. "For a moment there, I thought absence may have made your heart grow fonder, since we haven't seen each other in a few weeks."

Heat crept into my cheeks. "I'm aware our relationship has never progressed to its natural conclusion. You've pointed it out repeatedly."

"Then what's the problem? You're uh not..." He shifted on his feet.

"No, Clayton, I'm not gay. I'm convinced half my appeal for you—besides being your boss's niece—is the challenge."

He stuck his hands in the pockets of his khaki shorts and rocked back on his heels. "You know that's not true. Never mind, baby. I know that kind of talk makes you nervous. I just thought for a moment there..."

"When I threw myself into your arms?" I added helpfully.

"Yeah, pretty much." He grinned. At least the boy had a sense of humor...sort of.

"I am glad to see you." I'd be glad to see anybody right now. I tugged his hand out of his pocket and tried to lead him into the living room. "Tell me about your trip."

"Cut the crap, Cat. Why did you throw yourself at me?" Face set in stubborn lines, he pulled his hand back.

"Well, I was glad to see you." I nodded my head for emphasis.

"And?" He arched an eyebrow.

"It's impossible to wear down a banker-in-training," I groused. "Once focused, you're sharp as steel and about as malleable."

"I'll take that as a compliment. Now what's going on?"

"I thought there was an intruder when I was at the pool."

He straightened, all signs of the lazy playboy gone in an instant. "Why didn't you say so? Did you call the police?"

"And tell them what? A shadow fell across the pool, but no one was there?"

He gave me a strange look. "Is the alarm system on?"

"Yes."

"You stay here. I'm going to take a look outside."

"Thanks, Clayton." Relief swamped me.

"Stay here." He snapped the words out again.

"I'm coming with you." But I was already talking to his back.

I ran to the bedroom. He might have been conservative—okay he was conservative; he was going into the banking business. And he might not have attracted me at the basic level. But he was a good guy to have in my corner when the chips were down. He was no coward.

I rummaged in my dresser drawer for the Taser dad had given me when I moved out, grabbed it, and then ran through the house and out the back door in hot pursuit. When Clayton stopped abruptly, I ran full tilt into his warm solid back and nearly tased my foot. "Ouch." I rubbed my nose.

"Don't you ever do what you're told?" He eased me to his side, then cautiously walked the enclosure. The gray clouds had lifted. The sun dropped in the sky in a bright red orb that threw garnet sparkles on the water. A few early stars began to make their appearance. The scent of chlorine mixed with Clayton's expensive aftershave. I relaxed. No limes and cinnamon. The presence was gone.

We circled the pool and then the house. "I don't see anyone." Clayton took one last look around.

"Maybe it was my imagination." Not.

"In this case, I hope so." He glanced at his watch.

I could take a hint. "Why don't you go back to the party?"

"I'll stay for a little while."

"Really, I'm okay." Pricks of discomfort tightened my chest. I was so not okay.

"Tell you what. I'll take one more look around, then check the house before I go."

"Deal." My taut muscles loosened. While he checked the property, I grabbed a soda. He walked in as I popped the top. "Want one?" I asked.

He shook his head. "I'll just do a quick check of the rooms."

I swallowed a giggle. Clayton might not be getting lucky with me, but I had a feeling the evening wasn't going to be a wash for him. He went through the bungalow in record time.

He came into the kitchen and pecked me on the cheek. "I'll call you soon." He stopped me before I could trail after him. "I can see myself out."

"Sure." He didn't sprint for the door, but he disappeared through it pretty fast. I'd bruised his ego. Again. "I'm going to stop dating altogether." I'd never met a guy who melted me like molten lava, and I didn't intend to settle for less. "I'm a freak."

"That's the damn silliest thing I've ever heard."

Chapter 2

The scent of tart limes and cinnamon assailed me. I opened my mouth to scream so loud Clayton would hear me a mile away, which he probably was by now. Nothing came out but a dry croak.

The apparition stood in my kitchen as if he belonged there, tall, his coal black hair with a tint of blue sheen to it. He looked at me from stormy gray eyes that had a trace of devilment in them, partly hidden by bewilderment. The black suit jacket he wore came nearly to his knees. Beneath it, a beautiful silk, cream-colored vest covered a white shirt with a stiff standup collar.

"You can see me?" His storm-flecked eyes widened.

"Wh..." The spit dried in my mouth. I swallowed and tried again. "Who are you?" It came out a croak, but it came out.

"Your roommate's ghost." He grinned.

My knees buckled. Rear hit wood with a thump as I sat down on a kitchen chair. "Umm." I rubbed my posterior.

"I can't believe you can see me," he marveled.

"Yeah, me either." My heart banged in my ears. My clammy hands trembled. "If you don't mind me asking, what's your name?"

"Liam O'Reilly. And you are Caitlin?"

"Yes." I tried to get my breath under control before I hyperventilated. "What are you doing here?" I gripped the table and scooted my chair under it, so that the table rested between us. The muscles in my neck rigid, I concentrated on the pristine white ruffled curtains that framed the window and counted to ten before I glanced back. He was still there.

The ghost looked around the room and appeared as bemused as I. He glanced at my top, then quickly averted his gaze. I'd thrown on a black, cross-front bra tank-top over tan shorts. I watched in fascination as red stained his throat. It flooded his face and replaced the translucent honey-colored tan. His old-fashioned attire made my outfit look skimpy. I cleared my throat. "Um, what year are you from?"

"I died in October of 1866 in Ruby Falls, Virginia."

That accounted for the clothes.

"Now if I might ask you, what year is it?" He took a restless turn around the room.

"2015."

"Sweet Jesus," he breathed. "I beg your pardon."

"For what?" My brain, like my legs, had gone weak.

"For blaspheming." He rocked on his heels and added under his breath, "Just my luck I'd end up in a high-toned brothel after my death." He shook his head, his glance regretful.

Brothel? "Excuse me?"

"Isn't this a brothel?" He waved his hand around to encompass the room. "Of course, I've never been in the kitchen of a bordello, but I imagine they have them. This is the kitchen, isn't it?" He looked at the shiny stove, the spotless counters, and the black and white ceramic floor.

"Yes, it is. Why would you call this a brothel?" My knees unlocked, and I sagged deeper into my chair, more fascinated than frightened, everything surreal. I couldn't possibly be carrying on a conversation with a ghost. No doubt, I was in the middle of a dream, but I'd hate to see it end. Marcy's ghost intrigued me. For a man well over a hundred years old, he was a major hottie. The HDM paled in comparison.

"Well, you don't object to my language, you wear next to nothing, and you were in a very torrid embrace with that man who visited you a little while ago. Though to be fair, you did turn him down, and no coin changed hands."

No coin changed hands. Good one. "Times have changed." If this was a dream, it was the best one I'd had in ages, if I didn't count the sex dreams.

"Then I shouldn't be addressing you so informally, Miss...?" He arched an eyebrow, waiting.

"King. But Caitlin is just fine."

"Miss King." He gave an abbreviated bow. "I must say, your outfits are scantier than any bordello I've been to."

"And have you been to many bordellos, Liam? Or should I say, Mr. O'Reilly?" My insides warmed. I shifted toward the ghost, gave him a long look and my best sultry smile. Good Lord. Was I flirting with Marcy's ghost? Yes, it appeared I was.

"I'm nineteen, a man full grown. Of course I've been to brothels. But whatever era I'm in, this isn't a fit topic to discuss with a lady." Once again, his gaze drifted over my attire, or at least what he could see of it from across the table, his expression dubious.

"You're having a problem with my outfit, aren't you?"

"No problem at all. I like it very much." His lips tipped upward. His gray eyes sparkled like the sun on the ocean.

"You just don't think a lady would wear it." My throat tickled, and the muscles in my mouth twitched.

"Not in my time." He gave an apologetic shrug. "Though now I think of it, a grown man wouldn't go outdoors in short pants either."

That one took me a moment. I remembered the khaki short's Clayton was wearing and burst out laughing. "What a dream." I didn't realize I'd spoken out loud until he nodded.

"I feel the same way. Do you mind if I sit down?"

"Be my guest." I motioned to the chair across the table. It glided smoothly out from the table, and Liam drifted into it.

"Caitlin, who are you talking to?"

I jumped. Liam hopped out of the chair and stared at me wildly. Then he turned and bowed to Marcy. "Good evening."

"You must not have heard me come in." She walked to the refrigerator, grabbed a bottle of water, and looked around. "You're talking to yourself again, aren't you?"

"Don't you…" My brain turned to mush. I flapped my arm wildly in Liam's direction.

Marcy stared at my flailing arm in bewilderment. Liam looked back and forth between us, lifted his palms, and raised his eyebrows.

I regained my voice and my cognitive powers. I was having a breakdown. "What are you doing home so early?"

"Clayton claimed you thought you saw an intruder. I came home to check on you." She pulled out the chair Liam had vacated and plopped down.

"That was sweet of you."

"He shouldn't have left you alone. You need to find someone else. He slipped out the door with that Hathaway slut." She screwed up her nose as if she'd smelled something distasteful.

"We aren't an item."

Liam stood with his arms crossed, his face unreadable.

What was he thinking?

"Why do you keep staring over my shoulder?" Marcy twisted to look behind her before she shifted back toward me.

"Sorry."

"So why did you think someone was in the house?" She set down the bottle and leaned toward me.

"Must have been all that talk of ghosts." I bit my lips together to hold back the hysterical giggle lodged in my throat.

Marcy looked around, then whispered. "Do you think it was the ghost?"

My nerves jumped. For the life of me, I couldn't think of anything to say or why I was so hesitant to tell her the truth. She would have believed me. "Who knows," was all I could manage.

Liam looked relieved. Then his eyes crossed as Marcy's breasts lifted when she stretched her arms over her head. She glanced at her watch. "It's barely nine o'clock. Let's go to Jimmy's."

I looked at my ghost...er, Marcy's ghost. Would Liam O'Reilly be able to go? I couldn't wait to see his reaction to Jimmy's. "Sure, why not."

Marcy did a quick glance at my shorts and tank top. "Better throw on some jeans. The temp has dropped."

"Good idea. I'm going to do that now."

When I reached the bedroom, I unsnapped my shorts, thought better of it, and spun around. Sure enough, Liam leaned against the wall, his ankles and arms crossed. "Get out! I'm getting ready to change clothes. And don't go in Marcy's room either."

He grinned and gave me an appreciative once-over before he disappeared through the wall. Not so much as a ripple marred the smooth surface where he'd just vanished.

This couldn't be real. I'd just ordered a ghost out of my bedroom. I pulled my hair. *Ouch.* I was awake. And even though I had vivid dreams, I doubted if they included the scent of cinnamon and limes that lingered in the room.

I shook off my unease and threw on jeans and a pink tee, then shrugged into a pink and black plaid jacket and headed out to wait for Marcy. Wonder of wonders, she was ready.

We walked out, Liam at our side. When we got in the car, he balked. Unobtrusively as possible, I motioned for him to get in. He shook his head. As Marcy started the engine, I opened the door. "Just a minute. I forgot my debit card."

"Okay." She leaned forward and fiddled with the radio.

I jumped out of the car and jerked my head in the direction of the sidewalk. Liam followed me as I trotted back into the house.

"Where's the buggy?" he demanded, his arms crossed, chin jutted.

I desperately wanted to reach out and touch him, to confirm I wasn't hallucinating. Instead, I said as calmly as I could, "We don't ride in buggies. We drive automobiles. Come on. It'll be fun. You're a guy. You'll like it once you get used to it."

I was trying to talk a ghost into a car. What was wrong with this picture? I gave myself a mental head slap. On the other hand, on the off chance I was hallucinating, I might as well go ahead and enjoy myself.

"All right, all right," he grumbled as we walked to the convertible. I got in the passenger side and slid into soft leather. Feet planted on the driveway, Liam glared at me. I made a motioning gesture with my hand.

"What are you doing?" Marcy twisted toward me, a puzzled frown on her face.

"Fanning myself. It's not nearly as cool as you said it was." I flapped my hand back and forth in front of my face.

"You're acting strange tonight," Marcy remarked as she fastened her seat belt.

"I don't know what you mean."

"For one thing, the way you've been flapping your arms around like a deranged chicken. Never mind. Clayton has that effect."

Liam hadn't moved. I twitched my head to the left. Finally, he shrugged, put his hand on the side of the car, and leaped into the back seat of the convertible.

Marcy barreled out of the drive and tore down the lane.

"Holy Mary, Mother of God." The words were a whisper on the wind. I squelched a giggle, and Marcy threw me a perplexed look.

When her attention turned back to the road, I threw a quick glance at Liam. His jaw was clenched, and his fingers dug into the leather upholstery. He looked white as a ghost. The mental analogy hit me and I laughed.

"Did you break into Daddy's liquor cabinet?" Marcy demanded. She cut me a look before she turned her attention back to traffic. A jeep drew alongside. The good-looking guy in the passenger seat winked at Marcy before the sport utility vehicle zipped around and cut in front of her. For a moment, she lost her train of thought, but not for long. "Well?"

"Well what?"

"Did you bribe Lulu to bring you a bottle of Daddy's finest?"

"No! I haven't touched a drop. I haven't broken into Uncle Leon's liquor cabinet. And I haven't coerced Lulu to do so either." I huffed and flopped back against the seat.

Lulu was my aunt and uncle's long suffering, but well-paid, housekeeper who now had the extra duty of cleaning up after us. Marcy's parents had allowed us to move into their guesthouse until college started in the fall. No way would I screw up that arrangement by taking further advantage of their generosity.

"Hope you haven't been smoking anything. Mommy and Daddy would have a cow." Marcy pulled up to the stoplight and waited for the light to turn green.

"You know I never use drugs You've said yourself I'm so straight arrow I'm boring."

"No, what I said was it wouldn't hurt you to loosen up occasionally."

Heat burned my cheeks. No way was I discussing this in front of a ghostly stranger. I lapsed into silence before pulling my compact out of my purse and angling it where I could see Liam. Our eyes met. A sizzle of attraction jolted me right down to my sandal-shod toes.

I leaned my head against the headrest and closed my eyes, breaking contact. The whole situation was bizarre. My cousin had bought a ghost off eBay, and I was attracted to him. Whether he was real or a figment of my imagination, I was drawn to him.

Then again, what red-blooded girl wouldn't be? Even one who up to this point hadn't been tempted to do the mattress-mambo with any guy.

His thick hair hung nearly to his shoulders. His cheeks were high-boned and his nose hawk-like. Perfectly kissable lips. Not too thick. Not too thin. Yummy.

Before I could continue my inventory, Marcy broke in on my thoughts. "We're here."

I opened my eyes. With typical VanLier luck, Marcy had found a parking spot right in front of Jimmy's.

"I'd give my black and tan stilettos, and throw in my orange polka dot sandals if I could parallel park half as well as you do." The nose of the Corvette was a mere six inches from the bumper of the car in front of us.

"It's a gift." She waved her hand in an airy gesture and opened the door. The rose-peach polish glistened in the lamplight.

"Don't I know it."

Liam leaped out of the car and opened my door. I hurriedly put my hand on the handle to make it look like I'd pushed it open. I might as well not have bothered. Marcy was already heading for the entrance. In the blink of an eye, Liam was in front of her and threw open the heavy wooden door.

I swallowed a groan.

She turned to me. "They must have installed automatic door openers since the last time I was here."

"Must have," I said to her. "Don't," I mouthed to Liam.

He shrugged. "I'm a gentleman." As he held the door, someone came down the stairs from the tap room. He sniffed the air, and a look of rapture crossed his face. "Ale."

I sidled up to him and whispered out of the corner of my mouth. "Jimmy's is an Irish pub. Downstairs is for the under twenty-one crowd. Second floor, Jimmy serves ale and stronger beverages. Did you notice the separate entrances for the downstairs and upstairs?"

Liam nodded.

"Jimmy can sniff out a fake I.D. a mile away. By the way, can you drink or eat?"

"I don't know. This is my first time around. But I don't think so." For a moment, his sensual lips drooped before he shook off the disappointment and smiled. My knees went weak. "You'll just have to have a libation for both of us."

"Not at Jimmy's I won't," I mumbled in a low undertone.

He gave me a confused look. "Why not? And what is a fake I.D.?"

I slapped my forehead. "That's right. There were no laws against drinking if you were underage in your time, were there?"

"Underage?"

"No one under twenty-one can legally drink, so most kids under twenty-one try to find a way around the law, hence the fake I.D.'s. Marcy and I tried to sneak into Jimmy's once. Not only did we get busted, Jimmy called our parents. Just let me say, it isn't one of my better memories. There's nothing like disappointed parents to make you feel like pond scum. But even without alcohol, Jimmy's is always hopping," I said behind my hand.

"Did you say something, Cat?" Marcy called over her shoulder.

"I think there's an open table up and over to our right," I yelled back.

"Oh, yeah, I see it."

We pushed our way through the crowd to the open table. Marcy sat across from me, and her ghost slid into the chair beside me. When three men and a woman walked on stage, the crowd broke into applause and whistled.

"GRIT's playing," I yelled to Marcy.

"Cool," she hollered back.

The guitarist, wearing jeans that rode loose on his hips and a vest with no shirt under it, picked up his guitar, turned on the amp, and tuned up.

Liam clapped his hands over his ears, a look of horrified fascination on his face. His gaze traveled from the band to the young women who stood in front of the stage. His eyes crossed when a buxom blonde in a tight, low tee with hip-hugging designer jeans turned in our direction.

"There's Kendra." Marcy pointed at the blonde. She waved and motioned her over.

Kendra pulled out the chair that Liam was sitting in. Uh-oh. She'd barely settled in when she shrieked and jumped up, rubbing her rear. "Someone pinched me!"

Marcy rolled her eyes. "Is there a full moon tonight? Caitlin's been acting odd all evening and now you. The place is packed, but there's no one within pinching distance."

"I'm telling you someone pinched me." Kendra rubbed her right cheek.

"She sat on me. What do you expect?" Liam shouted above the music. Gentleman, huh?

"I'll take a virgin wine fizz," I told the waitress who'd stopped to take our order. Kendra and Marcy ordered the same.

As they chatted, I put on my rapt-attention face and let my thoughts wander. What was the matter with me? I'd been carrying on a conversation with a ghost as if it were an everyday occurrence. Why wasn't I locked in my room, shaking like a leaf? Or having hysterics?

Maybe Liam was the imaginary friend I'd never had.

The waitress returned and handed us our drinks, effectively breaking my brooding. She gave the table a cursory swipe with a damp towel, then left. I took a sip.

"What are you drinking?" Liam looked at my glass wistfully.

Marcy and Kendra were still chatting. I put my hand over my face and mumbled in a low voice, "Basically, a non-alcoholic fruit fizzy."

He looked down his nose. "A girl's drink."

"Guys like it too." Just then, the band stopped playing and the noise went down a few decibels.

"What did you say?" Marcy asked.

"I said the coolers hit the spot." I raised my glass. She raised hers and went back to chatting with Kendra.

"What do you think of Jimmy's?" I asked after making sure my cousin and her friend were still occupied.

He tipped his chair back, cupped his hands behind his head, and studied his surroundings. "Fascinating. Times have certainly changed."

I waited till the band started back up before I spoke behind my hand. "Thank goodness."

"Amen." He leered at a blonde in a low-cut plum top and tight Capris. *Men.*

Liam winced as the guitar shrieked. "The music's not exactly gentle or melodious. But it has heart," he added fairly. GRIT segued into a slow number while the soloist, Belamy Joyce, a young woman with blue-spiked hair, crooned about her brokenhearted lover. Liam nodded. "Now that's more like it."

A young red-headed guy with a stocky body tapped me on the shoulder. He leaned forward, cupped his hands together, and shouted over the noise, "Care to dance?"

Liam didn't wait for me to make up my mind. "Don't feel you need to babysit me. I'm going to mingle." *Poof,* he was gone.

Wow. My breath stalled.

"Would you like to dance?" the guy repeated, throwing his voice to make it heard.

"I'd love to dance." I preferred fast music, but if the band stayed true to form the slow song would be short. He waved a hand at his ear, signaling he couldn't hear me.

"Never mind." My chair scraped across the floor as I shoved it back.

We got to the floor just as the slow song ended. The drummer beat out a rhythm, and Belamy Joyce belted out a tune in a high shrill voice. The redhead shrugged his shoulders and grinned. "I'm Daniel," he said as he began to dance.

"Caitlin."

"Pleased to meet you, Caitlin," he bellowed as he waved his arms around and stomped to the beat.

I did the same, occasionally bumping into one of the other dancers on the crowded floor. After six sweaty minutes, the music shifted to another slow song, and Daniel eased me into his arms where we swayed back and forth in silence, my hands on his shoulders, his wrapped around my waist.

His hands dipped till they rested on my butt, and his lips found my neck. *Crap!* My muscles grew taut. I put my hands on his chest to shove him away when his head popped backward and his hands flew up, then flopped to his side. Wild eyed, he looked all around.

Liam stood with his hands fisted on his hips, expression thunderous.

"Someone jerked my arms right off you." Daniel's hand shook as he ran his fingers through his hair. The red strands stood on end in crazy disarray.

"Really?" I pushed skepticism into my voice and left him. I wound my way through the sea of couples to the table. Daniel stood in the middle of the floor, his head swiveling back and forth as he stared around him. With a perplexed look, he shook his head and headed for the bar.

I plopped down in my seat and looked around. Marcy was dancing with a handsome black-haired boy, and Kendra snaked her way toward Daniel. "Good luck and good riddance."

"Why did you let him touch you like that?" Liam glared as he towered over me.

My nerves were shot. No matter how natural it seemed talking to Liam, it wasn't. He wasn't human, in the flesh and blood sense of the word. I'd been conversing all evening with ectoplasm. And for him to question my morals? Me. Of all people. The only eighteen-year-old virgin left in Virginia.

"I don't need any lectures from a ghost on moral behavior, and I'm perfectly capable of taking care of myself," I shot back, before I noticed the girl at the next table staring at me. My teeth clicked together as I turned my back on Liam.

"Would you care to dance?"

My glance slid up worn, fitted jeans to a short-sleeved white shirt and a tan throat. It halted at an average-looking face with light blue eyes and thick chestnut hair that stood out in mild disarray.

He held out his hand, confident, his eyes filled with kindness. I slipped my hand in his, and he led me to the dance floor, drew me into his arms, and held me close, but not too close, actually moving in time to the music, not just swaying on his feet. "I'm Patrick."

"Caitlin." My throat was tight, my voice strained. Having a fight with a ghost will do that to you.

"I've seen you here before."

My head jerked up, and I narrowed my eyes.

He laughed, a low easy sound. "I'm not a stalker. You're just a very attractive woman. I'd have to be blind not to notice." He smiled when he said it and gained points by not tightening his grip.

"Everyone comes to Jimmy's."

He nodded in agreement. We chatted easily and continued to dance when the band switched to a fast number. Patrick was a good dancer and had a strong sense of rhythm.

There was no sign of Liam. Fine, maybe he'd gone to haunt someone else. Nonetheless, his absence made my stomach quiver and my nerves jump.

As the evening wore on and I didn't spot him, my unease grew. I tried to forget about it and enjoy Patrick. He was easy to be with, maybe because he was comfortable with himself. He seemed caring and confident with no pretensions, an unusual combination in a boy my age.

But no matter how much I enjoyed Patrick's company, I couldn't relax. I was waiting for a ghost.

About midnight, Marcy approached us on the dance floor. "Ready to go?"

"Sure."

She turned to Patrick and held out her hand. "Hi, I'm Marcy."

He shook it. "Patrick."

"Nice meeting you, Patrick. Let's go, Cuz."

"Okay." The room was packed, but no Liam. Nerves skittered just under my skin. The ghost was not my responsibility…regardless of how much it seemed like he was. I held out my hand to Patrick. "It's been a fun evening."

He took it and held it, his clasp warm. "I want to see you again."

"I'd like that." I tried to pull my hand away, but he held on and leaned in. Amusement danced in his brown eyes. "Would you give me your number?"

"Oh, sure." I rattled it off, heat climbing my face.

"Got it."

"Even without writing it down?" My neck cricked as I tilted my head up. He was several inches taller than me.

"Photographic memory."

"I'm jealous."

"I hate to break this up, but can we go?" Marcy asked, and shifted on her feet. She wrinkled her brow and scrubbed her forehead.

"Headache?"

"Big time."

"We've got to go." I eased away from Patrick till I was at arm's length.

"You're not in a relationship, are you?" He let go of my fingers.

"That's a very loose term for it." I continued to back up.

Marcy snorted, then winced and grabbed her head.

"You're involved with somebody?" He gave me a rueful smile, a look of comical dismay on his features.

"We're not an item."

"Glad to hear it. I'll call."

"Okay." Before I could say more, Marcy tugged me away. As we hit the door, I stopped and gave one last sweep of the room. *Where is he?* My pulse increased, and I started to panic.

"Come on." Marcy pulled me through the door. "Would you mind driving?" she asked, taking her keys out of her tiny black purse to toss them at me.

"Sure."

As we reached the car, my breath went out in a whoosh. Arms and legs crossed, Liam leaned against the shiny Corvette. The street lamp limned his high sharp cheekbones and sparked the blue highlights in his hair. Plain black cotton trousers framed long legs. My heart tightened and my bones loosened. He was just so darn pretty, in a manly-man sort of way.

His stormy eyes shifted to me. He stared, unsmiling.

The ghost was still in a snit. Well fine, I was in a bit of a snit myself.

We drove home in silence. I glanced in the rearview mirror. Liam stared straight ahead, his arms crossed, pensive. At least he wasn't white knuckling the side of the car. How strange this must seem to him.

I surfed the satellite radio till I found a channel that played old Irish ballads.

A beatific expression came over his face, making my breath catch. How could a man be so good-looking? Maybe it was a ghost thing. His expression changed to one of abject terror. "Watch out," he shouted at the top of his lungs.

I turned the wheel sharply to the right, just missing a little old lady driving a bright red sports car. She laid on her horn and stuck her third digit out the window.

Liam stared, his gorgeous mouth open. I think a senior citizen giving me the finger shocked him worse than my driving. After that, my attention stayed on the road, and I drove as sedately as a Sunday driver out to enjoy the countryside. Marcy snored softly beside me.

I hit the remote and pulled into the garage. Liam's eyes widened as the garage door rolled up. "Isn't that something?" He shook his head.

"Yeah," I whispered, then gently nudged Marcy. "We're home."

"Um-hm. Goodnight. I'm going to bed." She stumbled out of the car and into the house.

I collected my purse and followed.

Suddenly, he appeared in front of me, filling the entryway, his shadow dark and menacing on the wall. My heart gave a little thud. Should I be afraid?

Chapter 3

"I wish I could have danced with you."

Whatever I'd expected, it wasn't this. "I wish you could have too." The words slipped out before my brain had a chance to formulate them. Disturbed, I slid past him. "I'm going to bed. Remember the bathroom is off limits, and no watching while Marcy or I dress or undress."

"I'm not a peeping Tom." He drew himself up, practically quivering with outrage.

"And how would I know that?" My voice sounded weary even to myself, my shoulders slumped. Mom would have a fit if she saw my posture.

"Listen to your heart," he replied softly. He leaned against the doorjamb and studied me, his smile gentle.

"Don't say things like that. My heart's got nothing to do with it. I don't know you. You don't know me."

"What troubles ye, Caitlin?" His voice sounded like water rippling over stone, smooth and soothing, sliding across my senses like raw silk.

I shook off its drugging effect. I was too exhausted to be soothed and chose petulance instead. "Well, let's see. Could it be because I'm talking to a specter? Someone that's not real? Yeah, I think that's it." I stomped to my room and leaned against the door I'd shut with more force than necessary. "Well this has been quite the night. I meet a sexy ghost and a sexy man all in the same evening."

"I thank you. As for the man, he's an improvement over the other."

"Umph." I threw my hand over my mouth and swallowed a shriek. "This is my bedroom. What are you doing in here?"

There he sat on my bed, his black trousers and jacket accentuated by the ecru crocheted coverlet. The vest matched my spread to a T. Though, now wasn't the time to be considering ghostly fashion statements.

"I didn't mean to upset you by saying I wanted to dance with you. And I didn't mean to annoy you at the pub either." He rose and hooked his thumbs in his waistband, then rocked back on his heels. "You get as ruffled as my sister Anna." He grinned. The smile was short-lived as a shadow crossed his face. "This is my first time around as a ghost. It's strange to me too." He hunched his shoulders.

I didn't think the fact that he was a ghost had caused that brief glimpse of pain on his face. My tension eased as I tried to put myself in his place. Just the thought of it scared me spitless. "I'm sure it is strange. And this is your first time as a ghost?"

"Yes. I was in limbo until I got sucked into that test tube."

"You have—excuse me, had," I corrected myself, confused about tenses, "a sister Anna?"

He didn't answer immediately. Instead, he drifted to the window and stared outside. A fat yellow moon floated through the dark sky, a bevy of shimmering stars in its wake. Finally, he spoke, his back still to me. "Yes... I have a twin, Anna."

"A twin," I repeated. "I don't have siblings, but twins are especially close. Aren't you supposed to be linked?"

He turned and looked at me, the usual good humor gone. He sighed, a wispy lonely sound, and squeezed the bridge of his nose with his thumb and forefinger before he dropped his hand. "That's right. Linked is exactly what we are."

I tried to process that, but was suddenly too tired. "Where's your twin?" I held up my hand before he could speak. "No. Don't tell me. I can't deal with any more tonight. I don't understand any of this. And above all, I don't understand why I can see you when no one else can. In fact, I'm not entirely convinced you're not a figment of my imagination." I pressed my fingers against my aching head. I probably sounded extremely rude, but my psyche was on overload. "This is such a strange situation."

He gave a rueful chuckle. "It is, isn't it? If I'm a figment of your imagination, then you're also one of mine." He turned and gave me a strained smile. "And as far as why you can see me when no one else can... I'd like to know the answer to that one myself. But I can't say that I'm sorry it's you instead of your roommate—or anyone else for that matter." The heat in his eyes weakened my knees. An unexpected flair of response kindled in the pit of my stomach.

"I bet you were a bit of a heartbreaker in your time." I willed my thumping heart to slow.

He blushed.

Fascinating. Who would have thought a ghost could blush?

"The ladies and I got along well enough."

Heat rose in my chest and blood pounded in my ears before I realized what I was upset about. *You idiot, jealous of a ghost.* How stupid was that? I was beginning to feel like Alice in the rabbit hole. Another thought stopped me cold. Clayton was probably screwing his brains out about now, and the idea didn't even make a blip on my radar. Time to make it clear to him, we weren't going to happen.

I flopped down on the bed, toed off my sandals, and leaned back against the headboard.

He glanced at me. His gaze dropped to the cotton stretched across my breasts before he looked quickly away.

Heat flooded my face. Though why I should be embarrassed that he'd looked at my chest was beyond me. Guys checked me out all the time.

My cell rang. I rolled on my side and pulled it out of my pocket. "Hello."

"Hi, Caitlin."

"Patrick?" To have him call this soon caught me off guard.

"Yeah, I just wanted to make sure you got home all right."

A little ball of warmth shot through me. "I did, thank you."

"Sleep well then."

"You too. Goodnight." My bones light as feathers, I clicked off.

"Why were you talking into that gadget? You did that the first time I appeared." Liam stared at my cell phone suspiciously.

"It's a way of talking to someone by using radio waves."

"I don't understand." He shook his head.

"I'll show you how to use the Internet, and you can look all this stuff up."

"Internet?"

"I'll explain later." My lids were heavy. My eyes wanted to close.

"So who were you talking to?"

"Patrick."

"Oh." He turned and stared out the window.

A huge yawn escaped my lips. "Sorry. I'm dead tired. No pun intended." I fell back against the pillows. The scent of lavender from the linens vied with limes and cinnamon. "You smell so good," I mumbled, my eyes closed. The luscious scent of him grew stronger. I pried open my eyes.

He stood next to the bed, his head tilted, a small smile on his lips. "Sleep well, sweet Caitlin."

"Will you be here in the morning?" I closed my eyes again.

"If it's up to me."

I was fading fast. "Who else would it be up to?"

"Darn good question. Maybe we can figure that out, too."

The throw at the end of the bed slid over me. I snuggled into softness and warmth. *Too?* "Liam, about your twin…" Before I could formulate the question, I dozed off.

* * * *

A ghastly scream and the sounds of sirens brought me straight up in bed. The sky had lightened to a muted gray, but for all intents and purposes it was dark. I threw back the covers and stumbled down the hall to the living room.

Liam stared at the television as if he were witnessing the second coming and was afraid of his destination. The volume continued to escalate. "Stop pressing the button," I screamed.

"What's wrong? Why are sirens going off?" Marcy staggered out wearing a "Shop Till you Drop" neon-pink sleep-shirt with a shoe motif ringed around the hem. She squinted at the remote that floated in the air. I grabbed it from Liam and pressed down the sound.

When the reverberation had reached manageable proportions, I turned to Marcy who stood in the doorway blinking like an owl in bright sunlight. "Go back to bed."

"But the remote…" Befuddled, she continued to stare at my hand.

"Go to bed, Marcy. You were having a bad dream."

"Bad dream," she repeated, swaying in place. I started to throw the remote on the couch, thought better of it, and with a hand on her arm, led my cousin back to her room where she promptly burrowed under the covers. The sounds of her genteel snores faded as I left the room.

I walked to the great room. My ghost—I refused to consider him Marcy's if she couldn't even see him—stared in awed fascination at the television. "What in thunderation is that?"

"Television." I plopped on the couch and leaned my head back against the large soft cushions. "They had one at Jimmy's."

"I saw a box at the bar that resembled this, only smaller, and no magic came out of it."

"Oh, right. Band was playing. It was shut off."

"What is a television?" He reached out and touched it.

"A television is an electronic system that transmits pictures and sound. That particular model is high-definition."

"Television," he breathed. "Can I see the thick stick?"

"Thick stick?" I asked, my eyes drifting shut. "Oh, the remote. No, I'll just hold on to that for now. If you wake Marcy back up, I don't think she'll buy the bad dream twice."

"Remote," he repeated. "Show me. I promise not to hit the sound." He held out a hand I could see through.

I motioned him toward me, gave him a brief rundown, and dropped it in his palm. With a look of pure male satisfaction, Liam channel surfed.

"It's got to be imbedded somewhere in the DNA." I stretched out on the couch, pulled up my knees, and pressed my feet into the couch cushion. The first rays of sunlight filtered through the blinds. Might as well make some coffee. But I made no move to get up.

"Hmm?" He never glanced away from the screen, his eyes shining.

"Guys and remotes. Never mind." He sat at my feet. A low-level buzz of electricity from his nearness, as well as his signature scent of limes and cinnamon, gave me a strange sense of peace. I yawned and let myself drift back to sleep while Liam played with the wireless control.

The next thing I knew it wasn't cinnamon and lime but the strong aroma of coffee that tickled my senses. Marcy bent over me and waved a cup back and forth as she fanned the swirl of steam under my nose. "Wake up, sleepyhead."

"What time is it? Am I late for class?" I asked, groggy.

"You graduated over a week ago." She giggled, then looked at the television. "I wonder what's wrong with the TV." Channels flashed in rapid succession.

"Oh, my foot must be on the remote." My jaw tight, extremities twitchy, I sat up and swiped it out of Liam's hand. He grinned at me, stood up, and stretched, then slouched back down in typical male fashion. My irritation disappeared, replaced by warmth in the pit of my stomach as the fabric of his shirt hugged his chest.

At some point, he'd taken off his jacket. It lay carelessly across the back of the couch. The black, stark against the wheat and white tweed, shimmered like a glow stick. But Marcy didn't seem to notice.

"Here ya go." She shoved the coffee at me.

I sipped it gratefully. "Thanks. What time is it?" Liam stared at the screen with the sound down, entranced.

"Ten-thirty."

"Ten-thirty? What are you doing up? You hate mornings almost as much as mythical vampires do." Mythical till last night. Now…?

"It's Sunday."

"Oh, yeah, brunch with the parents at the manse."

"You're so silly. It's hardly a mansion," she said with the disdain of someone who grew up there. "I'm going to shower." She turned, then paused. "I had the strangest dream. I dreamt of sirens going off and someone screaming, and then I walked in here and you had the TV blasting."

"Really? Dreams are so weird." Though not half as weird as what was going on here. I clasped my hands around the warm ceramic cup and took another gulp of coffee. The caffeine rolled down my throat and kick started my system.

She shrugged and left.

Whew. I pointed a finger at Liam. "Stay." I tossed him the remote. "Here, play with the TV. Just stop if Marcy walks in, and for God's sake put the remote down if she does. I'm not sure what her reaction would be to seeing it float in the air."

"So where are you going?"

"Next door, to my aunt's house."

"Can I go?" He started to rise.

"Why don't you just stay put? Lunch with my parents can be challenging enough without throwing a ghost into the mix." The mere thought made my stomach knot.

"Whatever you wish." He sank back down, his gaze locked on the TV. He'd started to surf again. I pushed myself off the couch and went to get ready.

Fifty minutes later, I walked back in.

Liam glanced at me. His head shot up, his eyes widened, and he came to his feet. His gaze slid down my bare arms, shifted to my dress's fitted waist, then dropped to the flared skirt. The wonderful scent of him intensified. "Lord, you're beautiful."

I'd been told that before. But it never had the impact on me it did now. The intensity in his sea-gray eyes and the way he studied me, as if he could strip away the outer layers and see my soul, stunned me. "Thank you," I managed.

"Your skin glows like fresh honey." He reached out as if to touch me. His hand hovered inches from my arm, before it dropped to his side.

A pleasurable surge of energy danced under my skin where his hand had hovered. My breath lodged in my throat and refused to move up or down. I opened my mouth and pushed it out in a whoosh. "It's a good thing you're a ghost. If you weren't, I'm afraid I'd have to break my long streak of celibacy." Eighteen years, but who's counting.

His eyes narrowed in a male look as old as time. "I'd prefer doing the proposing, but I'd marry you."

My belly fluttered. "No one said anything about marriage."

"But you just said…" He shifted and turned his head a bit, a puzzled frown on his face.

"Times have changed. You don't have to marry someone to have sex with them."

"Well, that hasn't changed." He rocked back on his wheels. "You'd prefer to whore than to wed?"

"How rude." Heat seeped through my skin. "I didn't say that. Today, women are men's equals sexually. We can have sex with whomever we please with no strings attached."

"And is 'strings' a euphemism for marriage?"

Grin. "Yeah, I guess."

"And I suppose the short dress is acceptable in your time. Yes, it must be," he answered himself and gracefully left the marriage issue behind. Although the 'I'd marry you' certainly continued to whirl in my mind.

"Liam, the dress hits the middle of my knees. I hate to tell you but it isn't that short. Wait till you see Marcy. My cousin's dresses never reach past the middle of her thighs."

"I'm not sure my heart can take it."

I laughed and plucked a long strand of black hair off my arm.

"Talking to yourself *again*?" Marcy asked, as she came tripping in on three inch heels, wearing a pretty little square-necked, fitted pink dress that hugged her form and ended, as I'd predicted, at mid-thigh.

"Well knock me into a cocked hat. If that skirt were any shorter, her drawers would be showing." Liam stared in stunned surprise—albeit with a tinge of male appreciation—at my cousin's legs.

I giggled.

"What's the matter? Don't my shoes match?" She looked down at her polka dot stiletto strappies.

I shook my head but couldn't stop the laughter that erupted between my teeth. I bent over, holding my waist.

"Caitlin, are you all right?"

"Fine," I managed to get out and waved her off.

"You're acting strange. But then you often do." With her hands on her hips, her flawless brow wrinkled, she studied me.

"Pot calling the kettle black?" I straightened, still grinning but under control. I made a point not to look at Liam.

"Yeah, something like that." She grinned back, her humor as warped as mine. She took a quick look at me. "Didn't I tell you those strappy blue heels and that lapis and silver jewelry were perfect accessories for that white dress?"

"Yes, you did. Between you claiming responsibility for my fashion sense and Mom telling me I've got her legs, I've got nothing to call my own."

"Lucky for you, you've got me and Auntie. Now let's go. And Cat? No need to mention the ghost deal, especially since it turned out to be a hoax."

"You can count on me." I should tell her. Really, I should. But Liam was *my* ghost now. Plus, there was that little niggle of doubt that I may have lost it and was living happily in la-la land.

I gave a small wave. He lifted the remote in response. I hustled Marcy out before she saw it floating in the air. Shoot! I'd forgotten to ask him about his twin. I'd have to rectify that when I got back home.

Neatly trimmed shrubbery divided the manse and our cottage. A small break, cleverly cut out and maintained by the gardener, allowed passage between the two properties. A light, warm breeze carried the lemony scent of purple rhododendrons and pink azaleas that dotted the landscape. An orange butterfly landed on a pink flower, fluttered its wings for a moment before it flew away.

The sun mellowed the red brick of the two-story manse. Large white pillars gave timelessness to the home my cousin's family had lived in for five generations.

Our heels clicked as we walked across the wooden veranda. Before Marcy could open the door, it swung wide. Lulu stood in the entryway wearing a short black dress with a starched white apron and little white cap on her head. "Come on in, girls."

"Lulu, why do you insist on wearing that maid uniform?" Marcy asked. They'd had this conversation every Sunday for the past five years.

"Because your parents get a kick out of it." Lulu said the words as I mouthed them.

"Whatever." Marcy made a dismissive wave of her hand.

"Go on. Everyone's in the dining room," Lulu said as she shut the door behind us.

"Are we late?" I glanced at my wrist before I realized I wasn't wearing a watch.

"No. Vel got the meal together a little earlier than she planned and didn't want it to get cold, so she had me herd everyone into the dining room." Lulu shrugged.

Floor length white voile curtains danced at the open windows as we walked in. A soft breeze blew in the heady scent of hyacinths. The family was already seated.

"Darlings." My mother, nearly as tall as I, jumped up to hug first me, then Marcy. She wore a lightweight, cream-colored suit that showed off her still-perfect figure to perfection.

"Don't you two look a vision," Dad said from where he sat. Uncle Leon nodded from the head of the long gleaming table. Aunt Janet motioned us in, a smile on her pretty, unlined face.

We sat across from my dad and mom. The kitchen door opened, and Vel came in carrying a huge silver platter filled with fried chicken, mashed potatoes, corn, and rolls. The smells made my stomach growl. I could already feel the calories jumping on my hips.

"Pass that food around, baby girl," Vel commanded as she set the meat platter in front of Marcy.

Marcy forked a crispy, batter-dipped breast onto her plate and handed me the platter. Thinking of Liam and his fascination for short skirts, I took a leg and passed the platter to Uncle Leon.

Silverware clinked against china as the food made its way around. The succulent scents that swirled around the table made my mouth water. If I had a tail, I would have wagged it.

"Drat, I forgot the gravy. I'll be right back." Her starched white uniform rustled as Vel hustled back into the kitchen.

Seconds later, a high-pitched scream froze my blood.

Chapter 4

Chairs scraped and plates clattered as we raced to the kitchen. Her back pressed against the wall, Vel stared at a gravy boat that sat in solitary splendor on the glistening granite countertop.

"Vel, what's wrong?" Aunt Janet, barely five-two in her stocking feet, reached Vel first and put her arm around her.

"The gravy boat floated through the air." Vel's finger trembled as she pointed at the delicate china.

"Vel, have you been drinking again?" Uncle Leon ran a hand through graying chestnut hair, still thick and wavy.

Liam leaned up against the refrigerator with his arms crossed. "Reflex. She started to drop the gravy boat. I caught it." He lifted his hands in an "it wasn't my fault" gesture.

Sure enough, gravy had sloshed over the side and dripped on the counter. "What are you doing here?"

Dad, who stood closest to me, frowned. "What did you say, Cat?"

Liam glanced at Dad, then back at me. "I was snapped like a puppet on a string. One minute, I'm watching the news." His features relaxed in a sweet smile. "I love your picture box. The next, *poof*, I'm pulled here. Seems we can't be too far apart."

"Cat, what did you say, and why are you staring at the refrigerator?" Dad asked again. His gaze narrowed as he studied me. Dad was an independent reporter, a very good one. He hadn't won Pulitzers for nothing. When it came to news, he had the nose of a bloodhound. The last thing I needed was my father scenting a story.

My shoulders twitched. Nerves jumped under my skin. "Must be because I'm hungry. What's the gravy boat doing here instead of at the table?"

"Caitlin Lee, that's rude." Mom looked disapproving.

"Sorry, I was just making a joke." I brushed at a small potato lump on my skirt that had bounced from a spoon when we all made a dash for the kitchen.

"Maybe it was the ghost," Marcy joked before she clapped a hand over her mouth.

My jaw dropped. Liam and I stared at each other. He recovered first and had the audacity to wink at me. I frowned a warning. Though warning against what was a good question. No one could see him except me, unless he decided to pick up another gravy boat.

Uncle Leon turned to Marcy and sighed. "What are you talking about, darling?"

"Don't worry, Daddy. I'm getting a full refund," she rushed to explain.

"Refund?" Uncle Leon's voice sounded hollow. He tucked his hands in his pants and rocked on his heels.

At least my father had turned his attention from me to Marcy. The twitch between my shoulders eased.

"They had ghosts for sale on eBay, and I was the top bidder," she explained proudly. Marcy was such a riot.

"And what price did you get them for?" Uncle Leon asked, his eyebrows raised, his lips pursed.

"It doesn't matter. I sent them back. They were empty test tubes, and one of them was broken." She looked aggrieved. "The money should be back in my account next week."

"How much?" Though still calm, he'd developed a tic in his left cheek. Oh, dear.

"Only six." Marcy smiled brightly and brushed at her skirt.

"Six what, Marcia?" Uncle Leon only called her Marcia when he was on the verge of a meltdown.

Marcy cleared her throat. "Six thousand."

"You spent six thousand dollars on broken test tubes?" His low voice carried more weight than a bellow.

Marcy and I looked at each other. She swallowed and shifted on her stilettos. Before she could open her mouth, I jumped, figuratively, into the fray. "You can't put too high a price on a soul." I plastered a pious expression on my face, or at least tried to.

Uncle Leon gave me a pained look. "I understand this from my daughter. But I expected better from you."

"Why?" My mother shot me a withering glance. "You know these two have been partners in crime since they could toddle. If one was doing mischief, you could be sure the other was as well."

Partners in crime.

Guilt assailed me. I really should tell Marcy about Liam. At least I'd diverted some of Uncle Leon's wrath from her; I consoled myself.

My uncle turned to his only child and pointed his finger. "For sheer stupidity, you've outdone yourself. I expect your credit cards on my desk after lunch. I'll return them at the end of the month."

Uh-oh.

Marcy's azure eyes widened till they filled her face. "But that's over two weeks away, and there's a sale at…" Her voice trailed off as she took note of the alarming shade of red on her father's handsome features. "Of course, Daddy."

Her father swiveled in my direction. "And you, young lady, are not to pick up the slack."

I nodded. The word slack could be loosely interpreted.

"I'm sorry. I should have let the silly thing fall," Liam apologized. He had his jacket back on. His paisley cream vest fit his rangy body to perfection. The high-notched collar didn't look comfortable, but it did add a touch of elegance.

I nodded. At least this time I had the presence of mind to keep my mouth shut. My shoulders prickled again. Stiff as the proverbial board, I turned my head toward my father. Eyes narrow, he studied me as if I were a bug in a science project.

This was so not good.

Dad's gaze swung to the stainless steel refrigerator where mine had been moments before. Liam met his glance and straightened.

"I tell you that gravy boat floated through the air." Vel's ample bosom heaved. She stepped in front of Uncle Leon. "And if you don't believe me, you can accept my resignation here and now."

Liam looked alarmed. No doubt concerned about his gentlemanly gesture backfiring even further. The rest of us watched, amused. Even Dad's sharp gaze relaxed as he turned it on Uncle Leon and Vel.

The cook had worked for them since I was five. Not a month went by without some altercation between Vel and Uncle Leon. I think they both enjoyed it and, by my dad's twitching lips, he felt the same. He stepped into the breach. "Now, Vel. If you say the gravy boat floated through the air, I for one believe you."

In two strides, he stood beside her and put his arm around her. "You know that no one in the family could do without you. I'd be devastated without your Sunday fried chicken."

That snapped her back. *Clever, Dad, clever.* She straightened. "Oh my, your brunch will be cold. Go on in and get to eating. I'll reheat the gravy and bring it right in."

Uncle Leon rolled his eyes but trooped out with everyone else. As Dad walked through the door, he turned and stared at the refrigerator before he swung back and strode into the dining room.

I was the last one out. As I started for the door, Liam appeared in front of it. He raised his arm to open it for me before he caught himself. Either that or my look of abject terror clued him in. His arm dropped. "This is very frustrating for me. I'm a gentleman, not a churl. Gentlemen open doors for ladies."

Churl. I'd have to remember that one. The boy was fascinating.

"Go on, girl, before your father gets any more ideas. I'm right behind you."

"That's what I'm afraid of," I muttered.

Once at the table, I heaped my plate. My mom broke off her conversation with Aunt Janet, looked at me, and frowned. "Good gracious, Caitlin, you'll be sick if you eat all that. Are you nervous? You always overeat when you're nervous."

"Nervous? What's there to be nervous about? Floating gravy boats and ghosts?" Hysterical laughter burst from my throat.

Everyone at the table stopped speaking and stared. Marcy, bless her, changed the subject. "Momma, did you know Black's is having a shoe sale? Even though *I* can't take advantage of it, there's no reason for you not to pick up a pair of those darling espadrilles." She shot her father a martyred look that he ignored, and the conversation resumed.

After a huge piece of coconut pie, I rose groaning from the table.

"Cat, why don't you stop over this week? We haven't had a chance to chat in all the flurry of graduation and you settling in with Marcy," Daddy said.

Uh-oh, fishing expedition. "Sure, Dad. I'll bring Marcy along." *Check and check mate.*

I gave everyone the prerequisite hug before I hustled out the door, Marcy on my heels bemoaning her lost credit cards.

"Nice family." Liam floated beside me, his hands in his pockets.

"Mm-hmm."

"Not much gets past your father."

"Tell me about it."

"I just was. Weren't you listening?" Marcy stopped to pull a tiny pebble out of her strappies.

"Of course. It's going to be a long two weeks," I commiserated.

"An eternity." She sighed. "Just wait till I get a job. Then if he pulls my charge cards, it won't matter."

"Mm-hmm." I patted her arm.

"What's a charge card?" Liam's frock coat snapped in the wind, his thick tawny hair danced in the breeze. A lock fell on his forehead. He looked yummier than the coconut pie we'd had for desert.

My knees went weak. I raised my hand to push back that errant lock of hair before I caught myself. Finally, his question about credit cards registered. Pitiful. How had anyone survived in the 1800s without credit cards?

"You can tell me later," he decided.

Thank you, your highness, I thought, grinning.

Marcy glanced over at me. "It's not funny."

"Of course it's not," I soothed. Trying to distract her from her grievances, I asked, "You want to go for a swim?"

"On top of that dinner?" She groaned. "I'd never fit into my bikini. I think I'll veg out in front of the flat screen and watch a movie."

"Let me do a few laps to work off the potatoes and gravy." I managed not to look at Liam at the word "gravy"…but only just. "And then I'll join you."

"Sure."

We'd reached the cottage. She headed for her room and I headed for mine. As I stepped into the bedroom, Liam disappeared. "I hope you're keeping your word about no peeping," I whispered.

I tossed my dress on the bed, toed off my shoes, and slipped into my pink polka dot bikini, then swore. As bikinis went, it was pretty demure. It rode a sedate inch below my belly button and very little cleavage showed. The problem was my distended belly.

Marcy called that one. I thought about wearing my black one-piece, then decided against it, going on the assumption I'd swim it off.

I grabbed a short pink beach robe, took a detour to the fridge, poured myself some tea, and hauled butt out to the pool.

The scent of chlorine assailed me, and I dove into the cool clear water. Ten laps later, I dragged myself into a lounge chair and slipped on sunglasses.

The scent of cinnamon and limes tickled my senses. There he was. My heart gave a small jump and my stomach fluttered. How was it possible to have a physical reaction to a ghost, a mass of ectoplasm?

"You have a good, strong stroke." By the way his gaze traveled over me and the gleam in his eye, it appeared it wasn't just my stroke he liked.

He slid into the chair beside me, removed his jacket, and turned his face to the sun. His eyes drifted shut. A look of pure contentment played across his features. I had no doubt it was reflected on mine. I stretched out and wiggled my toes, admiring my Purple Sunset polish.

"What does your father do for a living?"

"Well there's a mood breaker." I picked up my iced tea. "He's a reporter."

"That accounts for it." He nodded his head.

"Accounts for what?"

"The sharp interest he took in me and in your response. Do you think he saw me? He kept staring in my direction."

"Good God, I hope not." I nearly dropped my tea. As it sloshed over the sides, I shook the liquid off my hand. A shower of tiny droplets spattered on the smooth white stones my chair rested on and splotched them with dark spots. "Enough about my father. Where are you from, Liam O'Reilly, and what are you doing here?" I leaned forward and sipped my tea.

"I'm from another time."

"Got that part, but where was your geographical location when you were alive? You mentioned Ruby Falls, Virginia. I don't think I'm familiar with it."

"It's a small town not too far from the Maryland border." He paused and raised his eyebrows. "At least I assume it's still there. My family ran a general store." He shifted a bit in his chair and smiled, as if at pleasant memories, and his eyes lit with mischief. "The sweets in the store were a nice benefit."

"So you were the kid with his hand in the candy jar?"

He threw back his head and laughed, a full, sensual sound.

"Did you have a happy childhood?" Sunlight and shadow played over his high cheekbones and chiseled features. He looked both ethereal and real.

"The best." He grinned.

Why did talking to Liam feel so normal? Feel so right? "Don't you find it odd that we are chatting like old acquaintances when we barely know each other and I'm flesh and blood, and you're ectoplasm?" How had it happened so quickly? The immediate connection. Nothing made sense.

He winced.

"I'm sorry. I didn't mean to be rude with the ectoplasm crack." I reached over to touch him. His gray eyes glowed, and his features grew grave. His outline grew sharper, more defined, and the wonderful scent of him became tangier with an almost sexual flavor.

"Right." I drew my hand back. *Stupid, stupid, stupid.* My heart galloped. What would have happened if I'd touched him? I rolled my shoulders and leaned back in the chaise. "So how did you end up in a test tube?"

"I have no idea." He put long, lean fingers on each side of his head and pushed his hair back. The moment his hands dropped, it sprang back. "One moment, I'm floating in darkness. In the old general store, I think." He wrinkled his forehead. "It's all very strange. It's like my room above the general store superimposed on a more modern room where people I don't know go in and out. I could smell the sweat and cologne of strangers, and the scent of my mother's laundry soap all at the same time. I was there and yet I wasn't. Not like I am now. It's like they were on the periphery of my consciousness.

"Anyway, the next thing I know some maniac, with hair standing all over his head and wearing glasses that are taped together, is clicking a little box that looks like a miniature camera. Every time he clicked, a green light shot out of the camera. Next, he turned on an apparatus with a hose that made a rumbling noise and, *poof,* I'm sucked down that hose into a cylinder bottle." He shook his head. "It was stranger than being dead."

"Fascinating."

"No doubt." He grimaced.

"I'm sorry. I'm sure it wasn't fun. But wow!" I remembered the second test tube. "There were two test tubes."

"That's right." His face lost all expression.

"Do you know who was in the second?"

He rose from the chair and drifted away. For several moments, he stared at the glistening water in the pool. Finally, he faced me. "Anna."

Chapter 5

"Your twin?" Poor Liam.

"What in the world are you doing talking to an empty chair?" Marcy had changed into white short-shorts and a fitted navy top. She looked both fresh and sexy. By the glazed look in Liam's eyes, he thought so too.

Inspiration hit me like a bolt from the sky or divine intervention—not to mention my increased ability to lie. "I'm trying out for a part in the local theater." B.S.-ing was an art form I'd always highly admired but never been able to master.

"Really? I didn't think you had any interest in the theater." She sank down on Liam's lounge chair. I opened my mouth to warn her but had no idea what to say. *Don't sit on the ghost?* Before I could formulate a plan, she sprang up. Liam had better not have pinched her!

He had a very satisfied male smirk on his face. When he caught my look of disapproval, his gaze turned pious.

"What happened?" I asked cautiously.

"I just got an electric shock. Have those cushions shocked you?" She rubbed her bum.

"Yes, now that you mention it," I lied again. Invention was the mother of necessity. Or necessity was the mother of invention. Whatever.

"I'm going to have Lulu spray those cushions with an antistatic."

"Good idea. Did you want something?"

"Oh, yeah." She snapped her fingers. "Patrick's on the phone."

"Patrick?" For a moment, my mind went blank.

"You know, the hunky biology major you met last night. At least that's what I thought you said."

"Oh, yeah, average face, good body. Yup, that's what I said." I pushed off the lounge chair and headed for the cottage. Marcy walked back with me.

Sandra Cox

Liam stood by the pool, his thumbs hooked in his waistband, as he stared into the water.

"Marcy, I'm going to grab my tea. I'll be right there." I trotted back, my sandals clopping against the pavement.

When I reached Liam, I leaned forward and whispered, my gaze traveling superstitiously around the pool. "Is she here?"

"Anna?"

"Yes."

"Unfortunately not. She escaped somewhere between here and Florida."

My heart gave a *ka-thump* of surprise.

"Cat, are you coming?" Marcy called out.

"Listen, I've got to take this phone call, but I'll be back."

"The guy from Jimmy's?" He rocked back on his heels, his face expressionless.

"Yes." I tried to gauge his mood.

He waved me off. "Go on, girl. Take your phone call."

I hurried into the hall and picked up the phone. "Hello."

"Caitlin?"

At the sound of his voice, tension left my body, and I returned to the world of the living. "Hello, Patrick."

"Did I call at a bad time?"

"Not at all." Liar, liar. Torn, I wanted to talk to Patrick, see him again, and I wanted to talk to my ghost. Was he all right? How did Anna's escape affect him?

"I had fun last night."

"Me too." I strolled into the great room, where the sun poured in through the window. With the cordless held to my ear, I drew the drapes before I flopped on the couch.

"I'd like to see you again."

"Would you?"

"Dinner tonight?"

I nearly groaned. I'd need to do another ten laps. "That would be great."

"Give me your address and I'll pick you up at seven."

I don't think so. I liked Patrick, but I wasn't giving my address out to anyone on a first date. "How about if I meet you?"

"Works for me."

We decided on a small Italian restaurant two blocks from Jimmy's. As I hung up, my nerve ends tingled, then settled as Liam materialized in front of me. "Don't do that." My heart had nearly crashed through my ribcage.

"Sorry." He sank down into the chair across from the couch. "So where are we going tonight?"

"We?" I didn't care for the sound of that. In this case, three most definitely was a crowd.

"Have you forgotten?" His fingers were locked behind his head as he leaned back in the chair.

"Forgot what?" I guess I had.

"Wherever you go, I go. We're linked." He stretched out his legs and crossed his ankles.

The look on my face must have given away my lack of enthusiasm.

"I won't get in the way. Besides, you need a chaperone."

A sigh started in my belly and escaped my lips. "Liam, this is the twenty-first century. Women don't go out with chaperones anymore. Do you recall seeing any chaperones last night?"

"Hadn't really given it much thought." He shrugged.

"Well, trust me. They don't. Besides, it's not like I'm a virgin or anything." Jeez, I was even lying about my virginal state to a ghost. For the life of me I didn't know why I'd brought it up, except for the fact I wasn't about to admit to a guy I'd never been tempted. It was just not cool to be a virgin in the circles I ran in, but I doubted if that was the case in Liam's world. I should have never mentioned it, and wished I hadn't, but it was too late.

I wondered if it would be any different with Patrick? I knew instinctively it would be with Liam, if he were flesh and blood instead of ectoplasm.

His breath caught, and he looked like I'd sucker punched him. My throat thickened. His fingers tightened on the ends of the chair.

"Are you a virgin then?" I asked rudely, going on the offensive.

"That's different. I'm a man." He lifted his chin, an affronted expression on his countenance.

"Oh, please."

"It's different." He placed one arm over the other and hooked them across his chest, his chin raised, lips tight.

"Not today, it's not." I crossed my bare legs. His glance followed the movement before he looked away. A trail of red climbed up his collar, then flooded his face. Intriguing. "I told you, women don't need to marry for sex. If they're involved in a relationship, it's a perfectly normal outcome." Well for most. I did a mental squirm. "Or if they want a one night stand, that's okay too."

"One night stand?" He cocked an eyebrow.

"You know, if you're attracted to someone and don't want any strings attached." My role of worldly sophistication, and the smugness that accompanied it, lasted for ten seconds.

"And what kind of relationships do *you* form?"

He sized me up. Disappointment flickered in his eyes, quickly masked. "None of your business."

"You're right. Of course it isn't." He disappeared. One moment, he was there and the next he wasn't.

"Liam?"

"Practicing your lines?" Marcy walked in, a can of soda dangling from her fingers.

Caught. I swallowed down my heart, which felt like it had moved up to my throat. "Hi, I didn't see you come in."

"What's the name of the play?" Marcy sank down in the seat Liam recently vacated.

"Ghost for Sale." My nerves jumped. Was that a masculine chuckle?

"Never heard of it. And while I think it's great you're trying out for a part, I'm off ghosts for a while. So what did Patrick want?" She picked up a fashion magazine and thumbed through it.

"We're going out tonight."

"That's great." Marcy clapped her hands. She was one of those people who truly enjoyed others good fortune.

"Where are you going?"

"The Grove."

"Good choice." She nodded approval before turning her attention back to her magazine. "You'd better get ready."

The jeweled tabletop-clock on the mantle showed four-forty. "Good grief, it's nearly five." I sprinted for the bathroom.

I took a hasty shower that left the room filled with steam and the scent of vanilla.

Figuring out what to wear, I paced inside the walk-in closet, looking for something casual yet sexy.

After tossing a dozen different outfits on the bed and constantly glancing over my shoulder to make sure Liam wasn't spying on me—though what the difference would be between my underwear and my bikini I had no idea—I decided on an ecru silk top, boxy linen slacks and strappy black-heeled sandals.

My watch with a shopping bag in the middle of the dial showed ten minutes till seven. Better boogie. "Marcy, can I borrow the car?" I called as I trotted out.

"Sure, keys are on the key holder in the kitchen." She'd switched on the TV, flipping back and forth from watching the jewelry channel to handbags. Sitting cross-legged on the couch, she munched on a bowl of popcorn.

"Thanks." I blew her a kiss.

"Have fun." She tossed popcorn into her mouth, her gaze glued to the tube.

The door from the kitchen to the garage opened for me. I was starting to get used to doors opening and closing as I approached. The Corvette's door swung open and Liam materialized. "You're a vision." His water-over-stones voice made my breath hitch. He leaned forward. "And you smell a fair treat."

"Thank you." I slid in the car and caught a whiff of cinnamon and tart limes. "You smell a fair treat yourself. I see you've got your jacket back on."

"We're going out."

That made sense. "About that, Liam..."

"Hmm?" He reached up and patted the dashboard. "I'm beginning to enjoy automobiles."

"Of course you are. You're a man." I backed the car out.

"Do you think I could drive?" He glanced at me, a hopeful look on his handsome face.

"Not in my lifetime." An icy shudder ran down my spine. "A car cruising down the road, with no visible driver, as if that wouldn't draw attention. Not to mention you come from the buggy era. But back to the going out thing."

"Um-hmm." Liam now stroked the cream leather seats.

Men. "Liam, listen up."

"I'm listening." He reached for the radio.

Forgetting myself, I slapped at his hand and felt a surge of electricity pass straight through me. Short blue currents of light shot up from the dashboard. "Ouch." I shook my tingling fingers. Now I had his attention.

"I don't know how this works, but I don't think it's a good idea to have physical contact with me." Regret flickered across his features but disappeared as quickly as it came.

"You got that one right."

"So what did you want to talk about?"

Finally. "Would you mind waiting outside? First dates are awkward enough without a ghost monitoring everything I say and do."

"You need a chaperone. He's a man. I know what's going to be on his mind." His jaw jutted at a stubborn angle.

"He's hardly going to jump me in a restaurant."

"You don't know him. He's practically a stranger to you." Disapproval radiated from every inch of his astral form. I'd noticed whenever Liam felt strongly about something his presence became sharper, more defined and he glowed.

I'd pulled into an empty parking space about half a block from The Grove. I faced the passenger seat, speaking to my ghost. "Well, I can't argue that. But I like him, Liam. At least, I think I do."

For a moment, Liam looked lost and oddly vulnerable. "I won't get in your way."

I leaned toward him but was careful not to touch him. "I like you too, Liam."

"Unfortunately, I also like you." He gave a short, rueful laugh before he pulled back. "We better go in."

I blinked, brought back to the here and now. Those stormy gray eyes could suck me in like a vacuum. He glided out of the car and, after opening my door, headed for the entrance.

There was little light in the dim entryway. The room itself was brighter. A middle-aged woman with graying black hair and kind brown eyes walked toward me, a menu clasped in her hand. "Table for one?"

"I'm meeting someone."

"Ah, the nice young man in the back I bet." She stretched her arm and pointed.

Patrick stood beside the table, smiling a welcome.

"Yes, that's him."

Liam walked through a few empty chairs as we made our way to the table.

"You look fabulous." Patrick smiled appreciatively.

"Thank you." Both he and Liam started to pull out my chair at the same time. Patrick dropped his hands and jumped back. Liam stepped back and slid into one of the vacant chairs at the table. "Sorry."

"Must be static electricity in the air." Patrick reached cautiously for my chair. When sparks didn't fly, he scooted it in.

The waitress took our drink order and moved away.

"So what did you do today?" Patrick leaned forward and crossed his arms on the table. The burgundy Henley he wore showed off a decent tan and well-developed pecs.

"Oh the usual, dinner with the fam." Calmed the cook down from a ghost sighting. "And you?"

"Dinner with the family." He picked up the tea glass the waitress set on the table and swallowed half its contents. She took our order and walked away.

After she left, I asked, "Who all was there?"

"Just my parents and my sister."

"You've got a sister?"

"At least we have that in common." Liam spoke in a quiet voice.

"I'm sorry, how thoughtless of me not to have inquired." The words spilled out before I could stop them. We'd been sitting at the pool and I'd let myself get sidetracked by the phone call instead of asking him about his twin, Anna. Remorse flooded me.

"Not at all, you didn't know I had a sister." Patrick gave me a puzzled smile.

"I should have asked last night." I should have asked this afternoon at the pool.

"Don't be silly." Patrick laughed.

I discreetly turned my chair so I faced both Liam and Patrick. "I'd like to hear about her."

"She's seventeen and driving the boys crazy." Patrick shook his head and grinned.

"Later," Liam said.

Whew. Holding up my end of the conversation would be challenging.

"I think I'll mingle." Just like that Liam was gone, at least from our table. My stomach churned as he glided into an empty seat beside two attractive young women.

"Is something wrong?"

The question jolted me back to my companion. "Why do you ask?"

"First you kept staring at the empty chair at our table, now you're glaring at those two young women a few tables down." He tipped his head and arched an eyebrow.

"I'm sorry. I'm just a bit distracted." Before I was forced to say more, the waitress came back with a loaded pizza. The smell of the rich spicy sauce left me weak in the knees.

Hot cheese dripped from the piece I lifted and plopped onto the plate. I laughed and bit in. Patrick followed suit. In between bites, we chatted like old friends. The evening passed quickly. When I noticed the busboys washing down the tables, I checked the time. "Holy cow, it's already ten o'clock. They're getting ready to close." I took a last sip of my soda and stood up.

Patrick drew his wallet out of his back pocket, threw some bills on the table, and did the same. "I'll walk you to your car."

"Okay."

Liam had been so discreet, I'd actually forgotten about him. He appeared at my elbow. "Time to go?"

I tipped my chin.

As we left the restaurant, Liam and Patrick headed for my car door. I shot Liam a warning look. He rolled his eyes and flew into the passenger seat.

"What a sweet ride." Patrick rubbed the side of the car with a lover-like caress.

"It's my cousin's." I slid into the seat and rolled the top down.

"Hmm. Maybe I asked out the wrong girl."

I grimaced, touchy about the subject.

"Just joking."

"Couldn't blame you if you weren't. She's the heir to the VanLier fortune." My muscles knotted, but my voice and my features were noncommittal. I hoped.

"Oh, Marcy is that VanLier." He nodded and leaned on the car. "Money is a great benny. But when it comes to a relationship, that's all it is, a benny. The minute I saw you, your head thrown back laughing at something someone had said, your eyes bright with life and humor, I knew you were someone I wanted to know better."

Warmth raced through me. I relaxed into the seat. Patrick was interested in me, not Marcy, not the VanLier fortune, me.

"No response? You weren't hit with the same bolt of lightning?"

Beneath Patrick's easy smile, there was a flicker in his eyes and tension in his shoulders.

Liam shifted in his seat.

Geez, I hated an audience.

I cleared my throat. "It's not that I'm not interested, but I'm not very good with relationships." There I said it. Mentally, I wiped my brow.

"There's no push here. Let's just take it slow and see what develops. Dinner tomorrow night?" He flattened himself against the Vette as a car rolled by.

"Careful!" My mouth went dry as the vehicle missed Patrick, though not by much.

He moved to the sidewalk and leaned in on the passenger side, near Liam's face. "Tomorrow night?"

Liam glared at him.

"Sure." His closeness to Liam unnerved me. Patrick angled his body toward me.

I leaned forward, my lips parted.

In the process, his shoulder rubbed against Liam's and sparks flew.

Liam jumped up, his feet on the seat, his hands fisted.

Patrick leaped backward, rubbed his shoulder, and laughed ruefully. "I don't know what it is about you. Till tomorrow."

"Tomorrow." I put the car in gear and pulled into the lane behind a blue minivan, then slowed for a red light. Liam slid down in the seat. He stared straight ahead, a pensive look on his face. I couldn't gauge his mood. "Do you want to take a drive to the ocean? It's only about twenty minutes away."

He smiled and my breath caught in my throat. Time stood still.

The car behind me tooted its horn, snapping me back to reality. The light had turned green. I tapped the pedal and the car shot forward.

In minutes, we'd left town behind. "Thanks for giving us some privacy," I yelled above the wind that whipped and pulled at my hair.

"Not a problem. It was a very informative evening," he shouted back.

"How so?" Since the lane was empty, I pushed on the pedal. The Vette leaped forward with a hungry purr.

"I had no idea women spoke so bluntly about sexual matters. Their conversation was bawdier than two sailors. Why they even discussed..." He cleared his throat.

"Yes?" I waited in fascinated silence.

"Never mind."

Laughter bubbled in my throat. I could just imagine that conversation. "And I'm sure you men never talked about conquests or a woman's attributes."

"Of course, but I didn't know that kind of conversation was reciprocated."

He leaned back, closed his eyes, and smiled. "I could get used to your mode of transportation. The wind on my face feels glorious. Though, it doesn't compare with a gallop on a good horse."

The unearthly beauty of him with his head thrown back, his hair flying as wild as mine, made my heart tighten. "You are so beautiful," I whispered.

His head came up and his dark eyes widened. "I thank you, but as I said before, you are the one that's fair beautiful, lass, with your long supple legs and midnight-blue hair. Your date had the right of it. You do have bright eyes and they sparkle like sapphire gems."

I bit my lip and laughed awkwardly. "It's not every evening a girl gets complimented by two gentlemen."

"By a gentleman and a ghost." An almost undetectable note of bitterness laced his voice before he lightened it and chuckled. "Perhaps that would be gentleman and gentle-ghost."

I gripped the steering wheel. It was too easy to forget my friend was a ghost, ectoplasm, not flesh and blood. "I had it right when I said two gentlemen."

We'd reached the turnoff to the ocean. I pulled off the main highway and drove a couple of miles to my favorite spot, a secluded inlet a little distance from the road.

I shut down the motor and relaxed against the seat. The waves lapped a soft rhythm against the rocks, the moon shone full and bright. Liam's luscious cinnamon and lime fragrance mingled with the scent of salt water and damp sand.

Wings flapped as a large bird, seeming no more than a shadowy outline, flew in front of the car. I pointed at it. "The bird is almost as ghostly as you."

He gave a soft laugh. "'Tis a very romantic place for a ghost and a beautiful young woman."

"A handsome ghost and a young woman." I leaned my head back against the seat and stretched out my legs.

"I don't know about that, but you are lovely to look at, lass."

I caught a faint hint of wistfulness that my heart echoed. If Liam weren't a ghost... But there was no point in going there. "Liam."

"Mm-hmm." Arms behind his head, he stared up at the moon.

"Tell me about your sister Anna. I should have asked about her before. It was just a bit too much, you know?"

"I grant you, it's not your run of the mill situation. What would you like to know?" The smile on his face faltered. He looked drawn and sad.

"Whatever you choose to tell me."

He shifted in his seat, his gaze on the moonlit water. "Anna was a beautiful little thing inside and out. When she loved, she loved with her whole heart. She was engaged to be married—just what is the proper age to marry for lasses in this day and age? Surely, you and your cousins aren't old maids?"

"Married! I'm only eighteen and Marcy's nineteen."

He chuckled. "Just teasing you, lass. You do want to wed someday, though, don't you?"

Someday seemed a long time off. "Someday, I guess. But for now I want to go to college, experience life. See a bit of the world.

"But back to Anna... Unless you'd rather not talk about her." Something about the stillness of him made me fidget in the soft-as-butter leather seat, uneasy.

He turned back toward me and gave me that smile that quickened my breath and made my pulse pick up. "You have only to ask and I'll tell ye anything ye want to know, including about my sweet Anna. How can I not? We're connected now. To my knowledge, you're the only person on this plane that can see me, hear me. I can't think of a connection more intimate."

I could.

He plucked a translucent piece of wheat from the air and began to chew on it. The thin stalk dangled from his lips. He pulled it out of his mouth and twisted it back and forth between his fingers.

Wow. That was some trick.

I refocused on his beautiful mouth as he continued to talk. "Anna had been in love with my best friend, William Donaldson, ever since she could toddle. She followed us everywhere." The smile crept back into his voice. He tossed the piece of wheat away. It dissipated in the night air. "When she set her sights on William, he didn't have a chance. That girl was more stubborn than Homer Winslow's prize mule.

"William considered her one big pain in the arse." He laughed and gave me a quick smile that invited me to share in the joke.

My insides warmed. His smooth voice filled my head and mesmerized me like the lap of the water against the shore. The night air danced and played with his hair. I watched his lips as he continued his story.

His beautiful voice deepened with sadness. "Then the war came and we enlisted. We weren't able to get home for two years. Funny little Anna had turned into a beautiful young woman. William fell head over heels in love with her. Anna was wild to wed him, but William had a stubborn streak himself. He was afraid she might get pregnant and he wouldn't make it back to take care of her. Still, he came to her at every opportunity."

In my mind, I could see the two young lovers clutched together in a desperate embrace, feel their pain of parting and fear of death.

"We survived, William and I, and came back home. Still, the lad wouldn't marry her."

"If he loved her, why wouldn't he marry her? That doesn't make sense."

"He wanted to get back on his feet. The war had ravaged the south, though we were luckier than many. Being on the Maryland border, our town had a lot of Union sympathizers, and we recovered quicker than most. Still, it wasn't easy.

"William got on his feet within a year. He'd built her a little house with a white picket fence. He even planted red and pink roses around it. They smelled as sweet as sin on a hot summer's night. I'd never seen Anna so happy." He paused and glanced in the direction of a splash close to shore.

I shifted in the direction of the watery sound. My attention soon drew back to my ghost. "What happened?" I prompted.

He drew a sigh from deep in his belly. "Southern boys went a little crazy after the war. Hunger will do that to you. A group rode into town the day of her wedding, wearing red bandanas around their faces, headed for the bank. Anna got in their way."

"Oh, Liam." My heart sank, and ice seeped into my bones. I rubbed my arms.

"She was in a hurry, not paying attention, and stepped off the sidewalk as they came thundering in. They rode right over her." Tension like thunder bolts filled the night. Electricity leaped and crackled in the air. Apprehensive, I checked for rainclouds, but the night was clear. The feel of an approaching storm came from Liam.

"I yanked the man closest to me off his horse and proceeded to beat the holy hell out of him. One thing led to another. I got shot."

A dark splotch appeared on his chest and grew in size, the edges ragged. My mouth dried and my stomach pitched. He glanced over, saw the horrified look on my face, and the stain disappeared.

"I saw this beautiful light, and I swear there were angels beckoning me. I started toward it, then heard a wail. I turned and watched sweet Anna rise out of her body. I reached for her hand, but she pulled away from me and started running toward the church, calling William's name.

"I tore out after her. By the time I caught up with her, the light and the angels were gone. Then we both fell into this black void. Sometimes in the dark, I could hear Anna calling for William. In the background, I could see shadowy figures as if through a veil. It was as if we inhabited the same plane as the living only in different dimensions. Then *poof,* we got sucked into those tubes.

"When Anna's cracked, she slipped out, looked straight at me, and said 'I have to find William' and was gone. Once again, I saw a bright light and angels and once again, I had to stay put. I can't very well move on without Anna. It just wouldn't be right."

"That has to be one of the most selfless things I've ever heard." My chest constricted and my eyes stung. "So if you weren't determined to find Anna and put her soul to rest, you'd be an angel now?"

"Well, now, I don't quite see myself as an angel, but I believe I'd be in the light."

"So instead of heaven you landed in what you thought was a bordello." For some reason this struck me as funny. Laughter bubbled in my throat and spewed out. It had a tinge of hysteria to it. I couldn't seem to stop.

"Are you all right?" Energy cracked. The sharp scent of limes and cinnamon intensified as he leaned toward me. I breathed him in. His presence steadied me.

I took another deep breath that mingled his scent with tangy damp ocean air and had an epiphany. "I know what we have to do."

"And what might that be?" He gave a puzzled laugh.

I leaned toward him. Excitement buzzed along my nerves just under the skin.

"We have to find Anna and William and reunite them."

"Well…" Before Liam could finish, thunder boomed, the earth shook, and a bolt of streaky white lightning hit the ground so close the air sizzled.

Chapter 6

Oppressive heat thick as molasses engulfed me. Hot air burned my lungs.

"Jeeze-us." The whites of Liam's eyes shone bright against the dark.

"Holy crap." I hit the button and the top rolled up. Sand spurted from the tires as I jammed down on the pedal and fishtailed out of the lane.

Back on the road, I realized not a single drop of rain had fallen. The pressure inside the car eased. "Well, what the heck do you think that was?" When Liam didn't respond, I glanced over.

He wasn't there! I checked the rearview mirror. If he was in the backseat, he wasn't in my line of vision. "Liam?"

The silence lengthened. My hands tightened on the steering wheel, and I slowed my speed. "Liam, where are you? I thought we were linked, that we couldn't be separated." Hysteria rose in my voice.

"We can't."

Taken by surprise, my foot hit the gas. The lights illumed the car in front of me. I had to pull around it or smash into it. Luckily, there wasn't a car in the oncoming lane or I'd be between the proverbial rock and hard spot. "Geez, Liam, you've got to stop doing that. You're going to give me a heart attack. Where were you, anyway?" I managed to ask after I'd caught my breath. I let off the gas and dropped my speed down.

"I went back to see what caused the disturbance on the beach."

"I thought we couldn't be separated," I repeated.

"I'm here, aren't I?" His voice held an edge to it I hadn't heard before.

"Yeah, but I didn't think we could be separated even that much. You must have been five miles back."

"I pushed against the link as hard and as long as I could till I was snapped back like a…"

"Rubber band?" I added helpfully, "Which is a circular, stretchy piece of rubber that holds things together."

"I know what a rubber band is." His voice had lost its sharp edge and now sounded dry. A smile slid into it, like the rustle of velvet. "It holds things together…like us."

"Yeah, like us." My insides went warm and fuzzy.

Up ahead, the lights of Faire twinkled in the dark.

"So did you find anything at the beach?" *Tap. Tap. Tap.* My fingernails clicked against the steering wheel, and I kept checking the rearview mirror. I let up on the gas as I hit the city limits.

"In a manner of speaking."

"Excuse me?" The hair on the back of my neck rose. A chill crawled up my spine. For a few blissful seconds, I'd managed to convince myself it was a dry storm.

"Something was back there. I could feel it. Couldn't you?" Liam asked. He straightened the cuffs of his shirt.

"I felt the air turn thick and clammy like a storm was coming. And then lightning and thunder. It had to be weather related." I held on to that thought like a lifeline.

"It wasn't the weather."

"What do you mean, it wasn't the weather?" Cold from the steering wheel seeped into my palms as I nosed the Vette into the driveway.

He didn't respond. I pulled the car into the garage and waited for him to continue. He rubbed a thumb against his lean jaw. A ghostly rasp from the five-o'clock shadow on his cheeks echoed through the car. His outline grew sharper, more defined, and his lips drew together in a straight line. "Something or someone took exception to what you said."

"What did I say?"

"I believe the gist of it was you were going to help Anna and William get back together."

Thunder rumbled inside the garage. Luckily, the bolt of lightning hit outside but near enough to shake the sides of the building.

"Okay, you don't need to tell me again." I threw up my hands in surrender from where I huddled crunched down in the seat. I whispered in the vicinity of Liam's ear. "What is it?"

He'd taken off his jacket. His heart glowed red and pounded a wild rhythm against the fabric of his shirt. A rapid pulse beat in his throat. He turned his head. His insubstantial lips were inches from my own. Pops of electricity snaked between us. I moved forward, all thoughts of the strange atmospheric conditions gone, my only reality Liam. Fire and ice shot through me, weakening my bones and softening my muscles. For the first time in my life, I wanted a man, or to be precise, a ghost.

The next thing I knew he stood beside the garage door that led to the kitchen, his breath coming in short sharp pants. He collected himself and moved back to the car. "Don't ever try to touch me."

"Don't you want to touch me?" I asked, hesitant. I'd never been brushed off before.

He leaned his elbows on the car and clasped his head. "Lass, if you only knew."

"Long dry spell, huh?" I surprised a laugh out of him.

"You've no idea. But even if not, I'm afraid your effect on me would be the same."

"Afraid?" I tried not to feel rejected.

"I'm very much afraid that no matter if I'm ectoplasm, as you quaintly put it, or if I was in human form, you would still devastate my senses. I've never met anyone quite like you. You're so vital and beautiful." His voice had dropped to a whisper.

My stomach fluttered. My lips parted. "This is insane. How can you exist and why am I aware you do? It's like we've crossed some cosmic barrier." I laid my head against the steering wheel, this time appreciating the cold smoothness against my hot forehead.

My scalp tingled as if he'd reached out to touch me, but the sensation was so short-lived I wasn't sure I hadn't imagined it.

"I know," he said in a low voice. "I knew you sensed me the moment I popped out of the tube. I saw it on your face. Why, I don't know, when no one else has. But I must say I'm very glad."

I raised my head and stared into intense, stormy eyes. His scent enveloped me. His nearness cooled my skin and scorched my heart.

"Maybe we should forget about finding Anna and William. I'm not sure I want you to leave." My eyes widened and I tensed. The last couple of times I'd linked those names together someone or something hadn't appreciated it. I looked wildly around. Nothing happened. Maybe whatever was out there thought I was backing off.

Nothing moved in the garage, the silence absolute. "Do you think it's gone?" A shiver rolled down my spine. I couldn't believe Liam's mere presence had made me forget there might be another entity with us. I cringed at the thought. What was I, a ghost magnet?

He closed his eyes and lifted his head. He stayed that way for several moments, then opened them. "The atmosphere doesn't feel as heavy."

"You're right." The knowledge surprised me.

"You said you didn't want me to leave." He stared at me. Those full firm lips parted. For one brief moment, it looked like he would forget his own advice about not touching me. Then my cell phone blasted, and in a blink of an eye, he'd returned to the door between the kitchen and garage...after opening the car door for me, of course.

I dug into my purse, held up my phone, and checked caller ID. I groaned. *Clayton.* "It's after midnight. What do you want?" I said by way of greeting.

"I'm sorry, darling, did I wake you?" He sounded solicitous and slightly drunk. The noise in the background and the slur of his words clued me to the latter.

"I'm still waiting for an answer. What do you want?"

"We really haven't had an opportunity to talk since I came back from Europe. I thought maybe I'd come over."

"You're wasted. Go home and sleep it off." I punched the phone off and shut it down for good measure.

"You shouldn't be wasting your time on that one. He's slick on the outside but shallow."

"You've barely seen him." I stuck the phone back in my purse. My ghost hovered a few inches off the floor, his arms crossed, a frown marring his perfect features. I slid out of the car, and we walked into the kitchen.

He leaned against the wall and watched me grab a soda. "I know the type. You deserve better."

"I appreciate your concern, but there's no need for it. I'm not interested in Clayton."

"Are you interested in me?" A second ago, he'd stood across the room. Now he stood beside me, passionate inquiry on his face.

"And if I were?" I fought back the heat that tried to flood my face. I normally didn't put myself out there when it came to dealing with the opposite sex, but everything about this relationship was different, surreal.

The silence stretched, broken only by the hum of the refrigerator. "Caitlin. Nothing can come of this. You're alive and I'm..." He looked down at himself and shook his head. "Let's just say we don't dwell on the same plane. You need a man, not a ghost."

My throat clogged. I swallowed down the lump in it. "But what if I want a ghost?" I whispered.

The hum of the refrigerator stopped. The atmosphere grew strained. "Then look me up when you die. But for now you need to find someone to grow old with."

My head jerked back as if I'd been slapped. I guess that's what I got for coming on to a ghost. What was I thinking? Well that answer was pretty simple. I wasn't. My hormones were. They'd been seriously hopping ever since Mr. Liam O'Reilly's appearance.

Up until the moment Liam had entered my life, I'd had no interest in having a sexual relationship. Now, I knew the old cliché about never having met the right man—or ghost in this instance—had the ring of truth to it. My longing for Liam was intense and painful.

I took a slug of soda and made a serious effort to compose myself. Pride came to my rescue. The ghost didn't need to know I had a bad case of lust for him and that his response of finding someone to grow old with had hurt.

He obviously didn't feel the same about me. Well so be it. I pulled myself together. "I'll do that. Though by that time, I can't guarantee I won't have changed my mind." I kept my voice light. "Want to go sit by the pool?"

A look of profound sadness crossed his handsome features. A moment later, the look of unhappiness disappeared as if it'd never been. "Sure. I like your pool. Do you want to put on one of the tiny outfits you swim in?" He wiggled his eyebrows.

"Uh, no." I bit my lips and swallowed the laugh bubbling in my throat. Human or ghost, boys will be boys. He might not want to linger as a ghost while I grew old and gray, but he certainly didn't mind looking at me now.

"Well that's too bad."

I ignored that and headed to the pool. I lay back on the lounge, kicked off my shoes, and wiggled my toes. A wispy gray cloud drifted across the sky and for a moment hid the moon. My silent companion had his hands behind his head and appeared lost in thought.

"A penny for them."

"My thoughts?" He turned his head and looked at me.

I couldn't decide which view was better: his profile that showed the high cheekbones, hawk-like nose, and the outline of bone and sinew, or the front with those stormy eyes and tantalizing lips. Oh yeah, had to be the front. I wet my suddenly dry throat.

"I'm thinking we need to move forward with our plan."

"Our plan?" Absently, I outlined one of the magnolia imprints on the puffy cushions with my finger, the material coarse against my digit. The silence stretched. The intensity of his gaze drew mine. Realization dawned. "Oh, to find—"

My soda left my fingers, arced into the air, and tipped into my lap. The next moment the can sat on the table. The cold wet liquid had me sitting straight up. "Urg." I jumped up and wiped at my slacks.

Liam raised a finger to his lips.

"Did you do that?"

He continued to watch me.

It took me a moment. "Oh." I sat back down. I had been about to say William and Anna. "For a gentleman ghost, that was most unmannerly." I thrust out my lip. "Being drenched in soda from the waist down is extremely uncomfortable." I grabbed a towel draped across the glass table and dabbed at my slacks, then threw it down and plucked the sticky material away from my legs.

"I'm truly sorry." He looked contrite. "But I'm afraid the alternative might have been worse."

My nerves, already raw, quivered and jumped. "Do you think it's dangerous?"

"It certainly has the potential." Features grim, he wrinkled his brow in a worried frown.

"Great." I flopped back in my seat, picked up my empty can, and set it back down. "Oh, right. Empty."

"Do you want me to get you another?" His shoulders hunched, he stared at the dark liquid puddled beneath the chair.

I brightened and almost said yes before sanity returned. Just the thought of Marcy seeing a can float out of the refrigerator to the pool turned me cold. "Uh no, but thanks anyway. So, do you have any ideas for proceeding with our quest?" Since he wasn't going to stick around to watch me grow old, we might as well try to reunite the lovers.

"As a matter of fact, I do. How would you like to take a trip to Ruby Falls?"

Chapter 7

My mouth dropped. "What? Why?" The light came on. My discomfort forgotten, I snapped my fingers. "You think we'll find…" It seemed to be okay to mention Anna's name as long as it wasn't in conjunction with William, but why take a chance?

"I'm guessing that's where she's headed." Apparently, Liam was being careful as well. "Never mind. It was just a thought."

My mind hopped like a frog. "No. No. It's a good one. But Marcy's going to Virginia Beach tomorrow, so the Vette won't be available." I jabbed at the air with my index finger as inspiration hit. "I'll call Dad— no, better make that Mom—tomorrow morning to see if I can borrow their car."

"You don't have one?" He stretched out his long legs on the lounge chair and crossed them.

"It's in the shop."

"It's broken?"

"Yes."

"What's wrong with it?"

He wasn't going to let this go. I cleared my throat and swallowed my embarrassment. "I had a little accident."

"Were you hurt?" He swung his legs over the chair and leaned toward me, concerned.

"No, just the car, and since it's a foreign make, I'm waiting on a part." I made a dismissive gesture with my hand. "Never mind my car. Like I said, I'll call Mom tomorrow morning and see if I can borrow hers."

"You don't want to ask your father," my ghost said shrewdly.

"Nothing gets by you, does it?" I laughed, then sobered. "You're right. Dad's like a hound dog. He can scent when you're not telling the truth or even stretching it. Let me tell you, growing up wasn't always a picnic."

"Your parents seem very nice, Caitlin." He toed off his boots. For a moment, his socks floated in the air before dissipating. He wiggled his toes.

Fascinating.

The ghost had long, elegant feet. Would I ever get a view of the rest of his anatomy? The clothes of his era kept him pretty well covered.

"Your parents seem very nice," he repeated.

"They're wonderful, but I never got away with anything."

He chuckled. "At our house, it was my mother."

"Parents," I commiserated.

He rose in a quick floating gesture and began to pace around the pool. My breath caught square in my throat as he cut straight across the center of it, the water sparkling beneath his feet.

"That's amazing," I breathed. "Even better than floating socks."

"What?" He stopped his pacing and hovered over the water. "Oh." When he understood, he moved to my side. "Caitlin, I'm in a damnable situation. I want to help my sister find peace, but I don't want to put you in danger."

A prickle of fear iced my spine before I tamped it down, impatient with myself. "I want to help her too."

He squatted down beside me. "Lass, you need to give some thought to this before you just jump head first into what could be a dangerous situation."

A light breeze lifted his shiny hair. I reached out to touch it before I realized what I'd started to do. My hand flopped back into my lap. "We don't know that it will be dangerous."

"No, we don't," he admitted. "But I hadn't expected the reaction we got to your plan tonight, either."

"That was a bit of a surprise. Who would want to keep them apart? Or have a vendetta against Wi—your friend."

The lamppost cast a yellow glow over the pool. Moths swarmed around the light in a crazy dance of death. My mind whirled with them, searching for an answer, while my body sank deeper into the cushions. "You talked about both of them, and there wasn't a problem until I mentioned—"

"Just don't say it."

"Right." I shifted. My pants were damp and uncomfortable. Even my underwear was wet. "Who did you know that had a crush on Anna?"

He stared at me. "A crush on Anna? Half the male population of Ruby Falls."

"Well that narrows it down," I groused.

"I see where you're going. You're right, of course." His eyes narrowed, and he tipped his head, an arrested expression on his features. "Lass, I could kiss you."

"Promises, promises." I flapped my hand in a dismissive gesture.

"If I had a bit more form to me, I'd take that as a dare and accept the challenge."

My breath caught in my throat. My tummy muscles loosened along with my knees. My arms rose of their own accord. His features grew more defined and his scent grew crisp. Sanity returned with a thump. I had to quit flirting with the ghost. I stood up and picked at my sticky slacks. A warm breeze plastered the material back against my skin. "Well, since I'm going to have to be up at the crack of dawn to catch Mom, I think I'll turn in."

"Good idea. Maybe I'll just surf the television." His eyes gleamed, and he rubbed his hands together.

Men and their toys. "Keep the sound down."

"Don't push the up arrow on the little stick. On the remote," he corrected himself.

"Very good." My ghost caught on quickly. As we reached the house, I didn't even bother with the door. Sure enough, it opened. I was getting way too used to this. "I'll see you in the morning."

"Good night, Caitlin." He picked up the remote.

"Good night." I trotted to my room, shucked my clothes, and crawled into bed. Before I could formulate any plans for the next day, I fell asleep.

* * * *

The rich aroma of coffee woke me. Its damp heat tickled my nose. "Thanks, Marce," I mumbled without opening my eyes.

"You are welcome."

I jerked upright. The sheet fell to my waist. Liam and the coffee whisked to the other side of the room, his movements so smooth, the coffee didn't even slosh over the side.

"You fixed coffee for me." A warm glow tingled somewhere between my heart and my tummy.

"I read the directions." He averted his face as we talked.

I'd slept in my white lacy cami. Thank goodness my thong was covered. I pulled the sheet up and tucked it around my breasts.

He gave me a quick glance, cleared his throat, and brought the coffee cup and saucer back. No cream. I took a cautious slip. No sugar either. I bit hard on my lips to keep from screwing up my face. "Thank you." I'd just slip into the kitchen and make it drinkable when Liam's attention was elsewhere.

"What if Marcy had seen that cup floating into my bedroom?" I shuddered. It didn't bear thinking about.

"She's sleeping like the dead."

I glanced around. My room was still dark. "What time is it?"

"Six o'clock."

"Six o'clock? As in six in the morning?" The cup and saucer in my hand rattled.

"Didn't you want to get an early start? I thought about waking you earlier, but you were sleeping so peacefully I hated to bother you."

"Don't you ever sleep?"

"I've been sleeping for over a hundred years," he reminded me.

"Good point." I set down my coffee, the better to clutch my sheet. "Now if you'd scoot on out of here, I'll get dressed. Thanks again for the coffee."

"You're welcome." He gave me the blinding smile that always made my breath catch before he turned and, without opening it, walked through the door.

"Don't think I'll ever get used to that." I threw back the sheet and made my way to the bathroom. Thank goodness the bedroom was an actual suite so I didn't have to go stumbling down the hall.

Once I'd relieved my bladder, I went into my little study in search of cream and sugar for my coffee. I pulled open the top drawer of my desk and grabbed a sugar packet and a small bottle of dry creamer, doctored my coffee, and sipped. "Ah." I closed my eyes as the warm sweet liquid coursed down my throat.

"Might as well get it over with." I picked up my cup and headed for the phone. My parents would be up and getting ready for work. I dialed, then crossed my fingers. "Pick up the phone, Mom."

"Hello."

Unfortunately the voice on the other end was too deep to be my mother's.

"Hi, Dad."

"What's wrong? Has there been an accident, a break-in? Are you in the hospital?"

"Of course not, I just wanted to see if I could borrow the car."

"Do you realize what time it is?"

"I didn't get you up, did I? It is Monday, isn't it?" Yup, we'd had lunch together yesterday.

"No, of course you didn't. We're getting ready for work. But what are you doing up?"

"I wanted to catch you before you left. Are you and Mom carpooling today?" I flopped down on the edge of the bed and studied my toenails. I needed to make an appointment for a manicure and pedicure.

"Why do you ask?"

Dad was in reporter mode, never answer a question when you can ask one.

"I already told you. I'd like to borrow one of the cars."

"Why?" he asked as I mouthed the words.

"I just had an urge to take a little day trip."

"Where?" he asked. Again, I'd known he would.

"Is it a problem?"

"No, I'd just like to know where you're going."

"Just out driving around, enjoying the beautiful spring weather."

"Caitlin, what are you up to? You don't honestly expect me to believe you'd get up at six in the morning to drive around and enjoy the weather?" His voice sharpened.

"Never mind. It was just a thought. I don't need to go anywhere."

"I didn't say no. I just asked where you were going. Of course you can use the car."

I figuratively wiped the sweat from my brow. I wasn't sure trying to reunite Anna with her lost love was worth the grand inquisition.

Heat tingled in my face. Shame on me. What was a few minutes of interrogation compared to over a hundred years of darkness? "Thanks, Dad. Bye."

"Be careful."

I clicked off, trotted to the bathroom, and took a hasty shower. It took me a while longer to figure out what to wear. I ended up in a pair of tan Capris, a fitted turquoise crop top with a turquoise flowered shirt over it, and matching sandals. Then I hurried into the closet and grabbed my floppy hat.

As I headed for the kitchen, the doorbell rang. "Who in the world?" I put my eye to the security hole and then flung the door open. "Dad!"

Keys dangled from his outstretched fingers. "I knew you'd have to take a taxi to our house or walk. Here you go."

A wave of love washed over me. I grabbed him and hugged him. "You're the best."

"Love you, baby." He hugged me back. "Got to go or I'll be late for work." He turned and with lithe grace jogged to the driveway where Mom sat waiting in the car. I waved at her and shut the door.

"That was nice of your parents." Liam materialized beside me.

"I wish you wouldn't do that." I put a hand over my thumping heart.

"Sorry. Are we ready then? By the way, you look lovely, lass."

"Why thank you. Just let me grab a cup of coffee and leave a note for Marcy." I snatched a pink to-go cup out of the cabinet and fixed my coffee.

"Ah," he said as he watched me. "Cream and sugar. I'll remember next time."

"It was very thoughtful of you to fix me a cup. I appreciate it." I smiled at him.

"You have a beautiful smile." The glow factor surrounding him ratcheted up a notch.

For a moment, I basked in it before I gave myself a mental shake and got down to business. I left a note for Marcy and scooted out the door to the car. Liam floated beside me.

"What is that?" Liam asked over my shoulder as I programmed the GPS.

"An electronic map. See, it tells us our route and how long it will take to get there. Just under two hours," I said with satisfaction as I pointed the route out on the screen.

"An electronic map," he breathed in awe. "Who would have thought of such a thing?"

"A geek." I backed out of the driveway.

"A geek?"

"A really smart person that's good with electronics."

"Geek," he repeated and nodded. "Are you a geek?"

I glanced at him in surprise, not quite certain I liked the question. I turned my attention back to the road. "Why do you ask?"

"Because you are an intelligent young woman."

"Well, I'm not that good with electronics," I evaded.

He studied me for a moment. "You don't like being considered intelligent."

"It's not cool." Uncomfortable with the conversation, I squirmed a bit in my seat.

"What does the weather have to do with anything?"

"What?" Then I understood. The chortle started deep in my tummy and erupted.

"What did I say?" He turned down the volume to hear my response.

"It's not the weather. Cool is an expression. An informal way of saying you're calm under pressure, graceful, look good, and you don't worry about studying," I finished comprehensively.

"Not worrying about your studies sounds irresponsible."

Unfortunately, he had a point. "You get my drift."

"Drift?"

"No. No more idioms for today."

"I know idioms," Liam said with dignity.

"I just bet you do, Ace."

"Ace?"

"Never mind. Tell me about Ruby Falls."

"It is—or was—a pretty little town. Cherry trees lined the streets and bloomed in the spring with a smell so sweet you'd think you were in heaven. And when the wind blew, white petals lined the sidewalk like flakes of snow." He settled back in the seat and smiled. "Our store was a two-story wood building on Main Street. It had a big glass window with O'Reilly's General Store painted across it in bold gold letters."

"It sounds like a lovely store. Where did you live?" I rolled down the window. The wind blew through the interior and whipped my hair around. One hand on the wheel, I captured the loose strands with the other, and stuffed it in the back of my shirt. "I should have brought a scrunchie," I mumbled under my breath.

"What's a scrunchie?"

"Saw that one coming. It's like a cloth-covered rubber band for hair."

"Scrunchie," he repeated. He was like a sponge, continually soaking up information about the twenty-first century. "As I mentioned, we lived above the store."

"That was convenient."

"Yes, it was."

We continued to chat. The sky lightened and traffic picked up. Fifteen minutes before we were due to reach Ruby Falls, I pit stopped at a local coffee chain for an iced latte, then buzzed on down the road. The cold caffeine surged through my system. As I approached Ruby Falls, I slowed. The population sign claimed twenty-five thousand residents.

Dread, thick and heavy as a wet fog, closed around me. What waited for us? An opportunity to send Anna and Liam into the light or a malignant spirit that would destroy us?

Liam shifted in the seat and stared around him. "Everything has changed."

Restaurants and small boutiques lined the streets, then fell away as we hit the historical district. I inched along behind a pickup truck. The town looked pretty and clean. As we passed the Golden Arches, my stomach growled. I turned on my blinker to take a right onto Main Street.

"Stop!" Liam yelled.

I slammed on the brakes and slid forward in the seat until the seatbelt grabbed and threw me back. Tires squealed and the car behind me laid on its horn. "What?" My heart did a wild ka-thump.

Liam pointed. "William's house." He leaned out the window to get a better look. "At least it hasn't changed."

"Jeez, you scared me."

"Sorry." His voice sounded distracted, his attention elsewhere.

I wheeled to the curb and put the car in park, then shifted so I could see past the ghost to the house. "He built a lovely home for your Anna. It's just like you described it, right down to the white picket fence and pink and red roses." I swallowed past a lump in my throat as I looked at the little house that represented the hopes and dreams of a couple in love, and a young woman who died before she could be carried across the threshold. "Did you want to go in?"

"Let's go to the store first."

He took one last look out the window as I pulled away.

Two blocks later, we were out of the historical district.

"That used to be the post office." He pointed at a savings and loan. "And that was the livery stable." He gestured toward a consignment shop with a green and pink awning.

"Lots of changes." I stopped at a red light. Two young women, with little ones in tow, hurried across the street. As the light turned green, I eased the car into the three hundred block of Main. Three-fifteen, three-seventeen... I counted the house numbers, then pulled in at three-twenty-five. "Here we are, Liam."

"It's not a general store anymore." He stared in shock at the old-fashioned two-story brick building. An elegant black sign with silver lettering read Gant's Hotel, 325 Main Street.

"I'm sorry, Liam." I so badly wanted to take his hand and give it a reassuring squeeze. "I can't begin to imagine what you're going through. This must be hard for you."

"Just a bit of a surprise, that's all." His lips twisted, somewhere between a smile and a grimace.

"Shall we go in?"

"Yes." He studied the building. "I thought this had been my resting place for the past hundred or so years. But how can it be?"

"If the ghost stories I've read are to be believed, it's possible. Didn't you say you could see shadowy figures as if you were on one side of a veil and people on the other?"

He nodded.

"Well then, let's go find out if you'd taken up residency here."

"And how do we do that?" As we studied the building, a couple walked out hand in hand, smiling.

My nails clicked as I tapped them against the steering wheel.

Liam noticed. "You do that a lot."

"Oh, sorry." I snapped my fingers. "I've got an idea. Come on."

"Where?"

"Inside." For once, I beat him to the door.

"What are you doing?" He floated beside me, his face alight with curiosity.

"You'll see." I patted my hair and put my best smile in place.

At the front desk, a tiny woman with gray hair curled around her elfin face asked, "May I help you?"

"Oh, yes." I held out my hand. My fingers engulfed hers. I dropped her hand, afraid I'd crush her fragile bones. "My name is Caitlin King. I'm an independent reporter. I'm doing a piece on hauntings in Virginia." I lowered my voice in a conspiratorial manner, and leaned in, my palms on the front desk. "I hear Gant's is haunted."

"Where'd you say you were from, dear?"

"Oh, sorry. I didn't, did I? I'm from Faire. It's a couple of hours drive from here."

"I'm surprised you've heard of us. The locals are familiar with our hotel's hauntings, but I didn't realize anyone outside of town knew our legends. I guess our guests have shared their stories."

She might be old, but she wasn't slow. "I've been doing a little digging, just enough to whet my curiosity, so I thought I'd come in person."

She gave an approving nod. "Enterprising, I like that."

"Can you help me?"

"I'd be glad to. I like initiative in a young woman. I've got plenty of it myself."

"I bet you do." My insides relaxed and warmed. I liked this lady.

She looked around. "It's pretty quiet. Let's go in the back. Would you like a cup of coffee?"

"Yes, thank you. That would be great."

She lifted the side bar. I walked behind the counter and followed her into a comfortable room. A coffeemaker and a dorm-sized refrigerator sat on an old scratched hutch. A blue couch and a blue diamond-patterned secretary's chair with casters faced each other.

"Cream and sugar?" She pulled two cups out of the hutch and filled one.

"Yes, please."

She liberally doctored my coffee with powdered creamer and sugar before she passed it to me. "Why don't you sit on the couch, dear? It's very comfortable."

I sat down, careful not to spill my coffee, then took a cautious sip. The brew was rich and fragrant. But, counting the latte, it was my third cup. By the time I finished it, I'd be bouncing off walls.

Liam floated around the room, eyeing everything. He studied a painting of pink peonies in a crystal bowl before he moved to a small landscape.

The woman sat on the office chair and placed it where she could see anyone who came into the lobby. "So what do you know about our hauntings?"

This could get tricky. I took another sip of coffee to give myself time to think. "Well, I've heard Ruby Fall's ghosts are a pair of star-crossed lovers from the Civil War era." A couple of them, anyway.

"My, dear, you're exactly right." She beamed at me.

Bingo. My senses sharpened.

Liam flitted to the chair where she sat and bent over her, his features sharp and defined, waiting. Her cup rattled against her saucer as she set it down and rubbed her arms. "My, it's chilly in here. Almost like the room upstairs."

"The room upstairs? What do you mean?" My pulse accelerated. I took a couple of deep breaths and forced myself to show a calm demeanor. She was chilly when Liam was near her. The room upstairs was chilly. Excitement skittered through my system. That room had to be where Liam had spent his last hundred plus years. Odd, that I seldom was chilly around him. Quite the opposite.

"One room is always cold." She rubbed her arms again. "There're never noises or sightings, but it's almost always cool no matter what time of the year. Now in the room next to it, our customers say, they can hear a young woman crying."

Liam began to glow like a neon light. He paced back and forth as if he couldn't stand still. He clenched his teeth against a visible tic in his jaw.

Goose bumps roughened my skin. "That must put customers off."

"You'd think so, but by and large folks are a bloodthirsty lot. They want to see or hear a real ghost."

"So it's just two rooms in the hotel?"

"Three actually." She took another sip of her coffee.

I wanted to rip it out of her hands and yell "tell me," but I remained calm, widened my eyes, and asked with the proper amount of interest, "Three?"

"Yes, we've got a very bad-tempered ghost. He limits himself to the lobby. I come in of a morning, and things have been moved around or broken. Nothing serious, an antique vase, flowers dumped on the floor, the candy dish knocked over, that sort of thing like he's petulant or spoiled." She sighed and shook her head.

"Interesting." I chewed on my bottom lip, trying to make sense of it. Surely, that wasn't William. And I knew it wasn't Liam. Maybe the malignant spirit?

"So, it's possible we have three ghosts." She leaned forward. "I think the star-crossed lovers are upstairs."

Well, that was one theory.

"I have no idea who the third ghost is." She glanced at my empty lap and frowned. "Didn't you bring a notebook or a recorder, dear?"

Oops. "If you let me, I'd like to come back. Today I just want to get overall impressions. Could we see the rooms?"

"We?" She gave me a confused look.

"You and I." I beat back the color that tried to rise up my neck. *Way to go, Caitlin.*

She unfolded herself from the chair. I half expected to hear her bones creak. I reached out to help her, but she batted at my hand. "That's a lovely top, dear. Where did you get it? I wouldn't mind one myself."

I swallowed the laugh that burbled in my throat. I really liked this woman. Her body might be aging, but her mind was as sharp as her bright, inquisitive eyes. She wore black slacks that bagged on her flat bottom and a bright yellow, long-sleeved blouse with a green ruby-throated hummingbird embroidered on the pocket.

"If you follow me, we'll just go upstairs and I'll show you the rooms."

We took the stairs instead of the elevator. "It keeps me in shape," the little woman explained as she pulled herself along the railing.

When we reached the second floor, we were both out of breath. Since Liam had floated along, he wasn't even breathing heavily.

"It's rooms two-ten and two-twelve on the right." A pretty, burgundy runner cushioned our steps as we walked. Old-fashioned yellow-flowered paper covered the walls. Lit crystal sconces mounted beside each door brightened the dark hallway.

We stopped in front of 210. She slid her card through the lock, waited for the light to turn green, and then opened the door. "That's strange. The room isn't cold."

A thought struck me and I motioned to Liam. He nodded and stepped up behind her.

"There it is," she said triumphantly. "There's the chill. It's odd that it wasn't cold a moment ago, though."

"Have you been up here in the last few days, ma'am?" The room had an oriental burgundy and turquoise carpet. Pristine white bedspreads covered the twin beds. A floral picture with a burgundy background hung on the wall and turquoise drapes covered the window.

"It's Aileen, dear. Aileen Blanchard. And no, now that you mention it, I haven't been up here in over a week. I'm surprised the maid didn't point out the temperature change. Prissy is a superstitious little thing. She would have talked about it if she'd been in here. Probably thought since there were no customers in this room she didn't have to fool with cleaning." She walked over and ran her finger across the desk and tisked. "Look at that dust." She shook her head. "Good help is so hard to find."

This had to be Liam's room. I tried for a commiserating look and suggested, "Let's go to the next room."

As she walked through the door, I whispered to Liam, "This is where you've spent your past hundred plus years."

"It appears so." He took a last look around the room.

"Did you say something, dear?" Aileen inquired from the hall.

The woman might be old enough to be my great, great granny, but there was nothing wrong with her hearing. "I just said this room has atmosphere," I improvised.

"Wait till you're in the next one."

Curious, I quickened my pace, then stepped inside.

Chapter 8

It dragged at my spirit. Sadness bled from the room, as if desolation had permeated the walls and flooring. Liam looked lost and miserable. My eyes filled.

"Anna," he called softly. "You've got to give this up and move on." He shook his head. "No, I haven't seen William."

"She's here?" I asked, startled.

"Yes."

"I don't know, dear. I've never seen her," Aileen responded simultaneously. "You can feel it, though, can't you?" She looked around the room, done in a similar style to the one we'd just been in.

"Oh, yes." I wondered if finding Anna would affect the link that bound Liam and I together. His twin certainly had the stronger claim. I decided to put it to the test. "Ms. Blanchard, would you mind showing me where in the lobby you get the most activity from your malevolent visitor?"

"Certainly." She stepped back into the hall.

I shook my head, signaling for Liam to stay with his sister before I hurried out, all but running in my haste to get out of that room. Ms. Blanchard pulled the door shut behind her. Good thing Liam could walk through doors and walls.

"Quite interesting, isn't it?"

"Very." My hand stayed on the smooth, worn rail as we trotted down the stairs. I didn't want to chance a spirit pushing me the rest of the way down.

"This seems to be where the spirit spends most of his time." Aileen walked right up to the front door and waved her hand. "When the books are knocked off, or the candy dish broken and candy thrown around, this is usually where it ends up."

"I wonder if he's trying to keep someone in or out. Or maybe both."

"I never thought of that. Aren't you the smart little thing?" She gave me an admiring glance.

I chewed a grin. The "smart little thing" was at least eight inches taller than Aileen.

"You know this used to be a general store."

"Really?" I came to attention like a pointer.

"Yes. There're pictures of the former owners at the Preservation Library."

"Pictures! I'd love to see them. Could you point me in that direction?" I wanted to hop up and down, and had to curl my toes and hold my stomach in to keep myself in place. Pictures of Liam, perhaps? Of his sister and his parents? "Can you tell me how to get there?"

"Of course, go up two blocks, then take a right."

"Thank you." I nearly hugged her but settled for shaking her hand before I hurried to the door.

"It won't do you any good to go today."

"It won't?" That stopped me in my tracks.

"Ethel, the librarian, is on vacation. She won't be back till tomorrow."

I slumped like a balloon with the air let out of it. "Well, thanks for letting me know. I'll plan on going there on my return trip. If it's okay, I'll stop by and see you as well. I'll even bring my notebook." I swallowed my disappointment. I really wanted to see those pictures.

"I'll look forward to it, dear. Have a safe trip back."

"Thanks, I will." I left the hotel, walked to my car, and slid in. "Where are you, Liam?" With a twist of the ignition, the engine roared to life. "Come on, Liam." Why did I have to try that stupid test?

Even though Anna had more claim to him, it didn't change the fact that I desperately wanted him with me. Being without him didn't feel right. How had I grown this dependent on him so quickly?

My chest constricted. I couldn't breathe. After a moment, I finally managed to push air out of my lungs and I eased into traffic. When I reached the stoplight, I was still alone. Tears welled up and spilled over. "You are such a sap."

"Here now, what's wrong?" Liam looked at me with the alarmed concern men through the ages have shown when confronted with female tears.

"You're here." I reached to hug him. Thank goodness the seatbelt pulled me back or else he'd probably have fried my circuits.

"Tell me what's troubling you, Caitlin." He leaned forward, his forehead wrinkled in a frown, his eyes bright with worry.

"Nothing. Nothing now." My heart sang.

"Did you think I was leaving you?" he asked softly.

"Yes and how crazy is that?"

"I'd rather tear my heart out than leave you," he said in a voice so low I barely heard it.

Somehow knowing the idea bothered him as much as it did me steadied me. I took a deep breath. "We've got to get you to the other side. You don't want to be a ghost the rest of your existence."

Silence stretched between us. Finally, he replied, "Here, I know you're right." He pointed at his head. "Here, I'm not so sure." He pointed at his heart.

My stomach fluttered. I cleared my throat. "So did you come voluntarily or were you pulled?"

"I would have found you, but it wasn't necessary, we're still bound."

The odometer showed half a mile from the store. "The distance we can be apart is less than a mile." I remembered the beach and amended, "Most of the time. Were you able to talk to Anna?"

"Yes and no." He sighed. "All she did was cry and call for William. She barely realized I was there. She's caught in the moment she died and knew she couldn't reach him."

"How horrible." I couldn't begin to imagine how hard this must be on Liam to see his twin in so much pain. "Do you want to go to your friend's house now?"

"Oh yes. If you park close enough, you can sit in the car and I'll have a bit of a look around."

"Works for me." I put on my blinker and headed for the historic district. Five minutes later, I pulled to the curb in front of the pretty little house and cut the motor.

Across the street, a head peeped from behind the drapes.

"Better make it snappy." I reached in the glove compartment, pulled out a dilapidated map of Florida, and pretended to study it.

Liam leaned over my shoulder. "I believe you're holding it upside down."

"Will you go?"

"Gone." He vaporized in midair.

The drapes twitched again. "Nosy old biddy, what's she think I'm doing, casing the neighborhood?" A face enfolded in fat and brown corkscrew curls disappeared behind the drapes.

Forget about her.

A light breeze blew through the window, carrying a faint sweet fragrance. My heart caught as I took in the riot of pink and red roses. I hadn't had a chance to study them earlier. They were an older variety that grew in a bush-like tangle, not hybridized like tea roses. Surely, they weren't the same ones William had planted.

A tricycle lay turned over on the sidewalk. Would Anna and William have had a brood of children if they'd lived? Would Liam have fallen in love with some local beauty and had children too? He would have made a good father and husband, strong but kind.

The slam of a car door interrupted my musings. I looked in the rearview mirror. *Crap.*

A police car sat behind me. A man in a blue uniform approached on the sidewalk. The old biddy must have called the police. She certainly hadn't wasted any time.

"May I help you, ma'am?"

"Hello, officer." I gave him my best smile.

He didn't appear to be much older than me, with cropped blond hair and blue eyes. He had red apple cheeks and an innocence about him that I imagined a few years on the force would wipe away.

He cleared his throat, waiting for my response.

Dad had always told me not to lie. He'd also said if I did to sprinkle the falsehood with as much truth as possible.

"I'm writing a book. Isn't everyone?" I gave a self-deprecating laugh. "I just finished talking to Ms. Blanchard over at the Gant Hotel, and I was on my way home when those gorgeous roses caught my eye. I pulled over on impulse to get a good view of them."

"We received a call about a stranger who's been parked along the street about fifteen minutes."

"Goodness has it been that long? No wonder the old bit...er, older person called it in. I'd better be moving along."

He grinned and looked younger yet. "Not much happens in Ruby Falls. You were a break in the monotony."

"I live to serve."

"Listen, I'll be off duty in fifteen minutes. Can I buy you a coffee or a latte?" He leaned against the top of the car.

I was being hit on by a cop. And if I had one more cup of coffee I'd implode.

"Thanks, but I'd better head home." I turned on the ignition.

"Will you be coming through town again?" He hadn't taken the hint but continued to lean against the car.

"Probably."

"Call the police station and ask for Officer Atwell. I'll show you around Ruby Falls. As small as the town is, it'll be a quick tour. But I might be able to help you with any questions you have." Finally, he stepped back.

"Thank you. I appreciate that." I put the car in reverse and just managed not to back into his patrol car. As I pulled out, I wiggled my fingers at him. He wiggled his back.

The nosy neighbor had her snout pressed against the window, a look of outrage on her features. I longed to stick my tongue out at her but remembered I'd crossed the shadowy threshold into adulthood. So instead, I waved. The drapes snapped together.

"Who are you waving at?"

"Will you stop doing that?" The breath that had caught in my throat went out with a whoosh.

"What?" He shifted toward me, perplexed.

"Appearing out of thin air."

"I'll get right on that." Sarcasm tinged his melodious voice. He pushed back into the seat and looked around. "What did the policeman want?"

"Oh, the nosy neighbor next door called me in."

"I think you've made another conquest. He looked smitten." He crossed his arms and frowned.

"Forget about the cop and the nosy neighbor. What did you find out?"

He heaved a sigh. "William is in the house."

"Really? Were you able to talk to him?" I braked as the light turned red, and Liam tumbled into the dashboard.

"Put your...never mind." There was no point in telling a ghost to fasten his seat belt.

He righted himself. "Aye, I talked to William. He made a bit more sense than Anna but not much. He kept repeating he couldn't reach her." Liam stared out the window, his expression pensive.

"This must be awful for you." I longed to touch him, to offer some form of comfort and couldn't. Instead, I took a firmer grip on the steering wheel to make sure I didn't do anything stupid.

"Harder for Anna and...*W*, I'd say."

"Did he say why he can't reach her?" I slowed. We'd left the small neighborhood and were back in the business district. Traffic in Ruby Falls was picking up along with the number of jaywalkers.

"He doesn't know. He just said he couldn't find her, couldn't reach her."

"Ha. It is the malevolent spirit keeping them apart." I forced myself not to bounce up and down on the seat in my excitement. "That's why the spirit hangs out at the hotel door, to keep William out. Speaking of the malevolent spirit, did you see anything when we were at the hotel?" A small boutique on my left had a shoe sale sign in the window. I straightened my shoulders and forced myself to keep driving. Sometimes sacrifices had to be made for the good of the cause.

"No. I've never picked up on it, except when you mentioned reuniting you know who with you know who. I guess that makes me an unobservant ghost." He grimaced.

"Odd. We've got a malicious spirit that tosses the hotel lobby but doesn't bother you until you've both been freed. Of course, he didn't need to. Anna wasn't in any danger of finding W, because she was stuck in the moment of her death. Well, not her death precisely, but directly after when she knew she wouldn't be with W. And by guarding the door he's managed to keep W out," I told Liam, proud of myself for not using William's name out loud. "Why did Anna go back home?"

"She's waiting for William to find her." Liam sighed and settled back into the seat, though one hand remained on the dashboard as if prepared to brace himself.

The situation was unbearably sad. My heart hurt for all three of them. "I wonder how we can get them together."

"I wish I knew." Liam scratched his chin. It had a dark look to it, as if he had a heavy beard. I could have sworn the gesture produced a raspy sound like a hand rubbing whiskers. "Whoever it is, he's managed to throw a barrier up between them."

"So why do I upset him? Why hasn't he appeared before? Though he's apparently thrown temper tantrums in the past from what Aileen described."

"You're the unknown element. A human. He probably has no idea what you're capable of."

"Makes sense."

My mind humming, I tapped my fingers against the steering wheel. "So tell me again what W said about trying to see Anna."

"He said he couldn't find her. Couldn't reach her."

Excitement rose in my throat and bubbled out my mouth. "Has he been to the hotel?"

"He didn't say. Is it important?"

"I don't know. Maybe, maybe not. But any information we can get at this point has got to help us, bring us one step closer to solving the puzzle."

I took a quick look around, jerked the wheel, and made a U turn. Liam grabbed the door handle to keep from landing in my lap. "What in the name of all that's holy are you doing?"

"Going back to see William. Let's find out if he's been to the hotel. I'm betting he has, that he's the reason the place is getting trashed. And if he has, what are the parameters? How close can he get to her?" I gave him a sideways glance. "And maybe with the two of you together, he can make it to her side."

"You're brilliant, lass." His smile brightened the car's interior as he caught my excitement.

"We'll see if I'm brilliant or not. I can't park in front of the house because of the nosy neighbor. Any ideas?"

"There used to be an alley out back. Let's try that."

I cut over a block and then up. I looked around uneasily. William's house was nice and in the historical district. This area might have been nice at one time, but right now it made my skin crawl.

"This may not be such a good idea. It's not like I remember," he said as the car inched down the narrow, dark alley.

"Don't worry. I'll be fine. If I get in any trouble, I'll just leave and drive around the block. If the old biddy sees me, she sees me." I shrugged.

"Lock the door."

"Right." I pressed the locks down.

"So, you'll find out if William has been to the hotel and if he's willing to go back with you. Right?"

He nodded.

"If he is, we'll go back and see how the other ghost does against the both of you."

"Yes. Be careful. At the least sign of trouble, you leave." *Whoosh.* He was gone.

The car running, I checked my phone for messages, then fiddled with the radio.

"Crap." The rearview mirror showed two young men with baggy pants and straggly hair approaching. I turned down the music.

The men flanked the car. Nerves crawled up my spine.

The guy on my side leaned against the door and circled with his finger. "Roll down the window, pretty momma." He was close enough I could hear him through the glass.

I shook my head.

"Now that's not very friendly."

The other one rattled the door handle.

"Oh great, where's a policeman when you need him," I muttered.

"Come on." The one on my side smiled and winked.

All I've got to do is stall them. I stared straight ahead. As he pounded his palm against the window, my chest tightened and my heart raced.

He stepped back and suddenly the car began to rock. The young hoodlums giggled hysterically as they pushed the car back and forth between them. As heat shot through me, my fear disappeared. "Hey, you jerks, cut it out!" They laughed and continued to rock the car.

I laid on the horn.

The rocking stopped. The guy on my side glared at me, and I glared back until he pulled out a knife and started toward my tires.

"Don't you dare!" I pushed open the door, hoping to knock him flat.

The door slammed shut, and the knife went flying through the air as Liam shoved him backward. The punk stumbled and looked wildly around. "What the hell?"

"What's wrong with you, Jake?" his friend yelled.

Jake batted his hands, then turned to run. "Let's get out of here."

Liam put a well-placed boot to his rear and moved him along even quicker. Jake stumbled and took off running, his sidekick trotting after him, looking back in a bewildered fashion.

Liam glided into the car, his expression grim. "Let's go."

I backed the car down the alley. My two antagonists disappeared around the corner in the opposite direction.

"Thanks for that." My muscles loosened and my breath whished out.

Liam didn't respond. His features were sharp and defined to the point he was practically glowing.

"Are you okay?"

"Jeez-us, girl, what were you thinking? You could have been seriously hurt back there. Honking the horn was smart. What made you get out of the car?"

"They were going to slash my tires."

"Better your tires than your throat." His arms were crossed, and his features looked like a thunderstorm about to break. Waves of disapproval radiated off him.

"Maybe you're right," I conceded.

"Maybe?"

"For the sake of argument, let's say you are right. I just lost it, okay? It was stupid. I'm sorry."

He sighed. "Caitlin, if something happened to you, I don't think I could bear it. Just have a care, all right?"

I threw him a quick smile. "Most certainly. What did you find out?"

He accepted the change in conversation. "You were right. He can get as far as opening the door to the lobby; then he's met with a force field he can't get past."

"So he knew Anna was there?"

"No, not for sure. It just seemed, to him, to be the logical place she'd be."

"Why do you suppose he can move around and you and Anna haven't been able to until recently?"

"Good question." He thrummed his fingers on the side of the car. "I don't know. Maybe it's got something to do with our deaths. Mine and Anna's were violent." He lifted and dropped his shoulders. "He's locked in the past and almost never ventures from the house he built for her. He thinks she'll come to him."

"And she thinks he'll come to her." Pity surged through me and my eyelids heated. I blinked back moisture. "Well we are going to do something about that."

"Yes, we are. William and I will check out the hotel."

"You aren't leaving me out of this!"

"Be reasonable, lass. You'll make Miss Aileen suspicious."

"What am I supposed to do?"

"I saw an ice cream parlor a block down. Why don't you wait for me there?"

We'd reached the hotel. Against my better judgment, I drove past. "Pat me on the head and buy me ice cream. What am I, two years old?" I grumbled.

As I pulled into a parking spot in front of an old-fashioned ice cream parlor, I caught him biting back a smile.

"It's not funny. I should be going with you. And if it wasn't for the fact I probably would make Aileen suspicious, I'd do just that."

He reached his hand in the direction of my hair, then dropped it. "Lass, my heart stopped when I saw that hooligan with a knife. Let's not tempt fate. I don't want you around whatever is keeping Anna and…" He cleared his throat. "Apart. Humans are frail and damage easily."

"What if it hurts you?"

He shrugged his shoulders. "What can it do to me? I'll be back soon."

And like that, he was gone. My insides were churning. Maybe ice cream wasn't a bad idea after all. A bell tinkled cheerfully as I opened the door. I walked to the counter and ordered a large hot-fudge sundae with whipped cream, nuts, and a cherry. Two bites into the sinful, warm sauce and my equilibrium righted. By the time Liam returned I had finished the ice cream and was licking the spoon. As soon as I saw him, I jumped up and hurried outside. "Well?" I demanded once we were inside the car.

He shook his head. "Even with the two of us together, we couldn't break through the barrier. We got to the base of the stairs, which is farther than William said he's ever got, and then things started flying through the air, and we decided we'd better leave."

"Was anyone hurt?" Nerves thrummed through me.

"No. Thank goodness, no one was in the lobby. It was a good idea, lass. But whatever force is keeping us out, it's stronger than both of us."

"No point in trying again?"

"No, it's not the way to combat it. We've got to think of something else."

"Okay, then that's what we'll do."

He smiled. "That's one of the many things I…like about you."

My tummy tingled. *Had he been about to say love?*

"You never give up and you never get discouraged."

"Well that may be a slight exaggeration, but I don't plan on giving up on this."

As we left town, my cell phone rang. I reached for it with one hand, my other on the steering wheel.

"Maybe you should take that later." Liam glanced at the phone, then at the road.

"I'm okay." Before he could object further, I answered the phone. "Hello."

"Hi, Caitlin."

"Hi, Patrick." Tension left my body. The realm of the supernatural was replaced by the here and now, and sunshine.

"What are you up to?"

Tracking down ghosts. "If I tell you, don't laugh."

"I probably won't."

"I like that about you. You don't promise what you can't deliver. Did I mention I'm planning on majoring in Journalism?" As of just this moment. Though the seed had been planted long ago.

"No, you didn't. And this has a bearing on what you're doing?"

"Right." The wind blew through the open window and whipped my hair in my eyes. But I didn't have a free hand to get it out of my face.

A mild electrical current rippled across my face as my hair was tucked behind my ear. Liam eased back in his seat.

"Sorry," he muttered. "I shouldn't have done that."

I yelped and dropped the phone face down on my lap, which is what I should have done in the first place. "Thanks." I still tingled. I took a quick glance in the mirror, at least my hair wasn't standing on end or singed.

I picked up the phone. "Patrick, I'll call you back." As soon as I saw a rest area, I pulled in. A couple dozen cars were in the parking lot. Several people walked their dogs. Others ambled toward the restrooms or the vending machines.

I hit redial.

"Caitlin?"

"Sorry, I was trying to drive on the road and had to pull over."

"Are you okay?"

"Yeah, I'm fine." Just a little shocked.

"You're sure you're okay?"

"I'm fine."

"You screeched."

"No, I didn't."

"Okay. So what were you saying before you didn't screech."

"Funny guy. I was saying I'm researching ghosts in Virginia. If I can get some decent material, I'll write an article and turn it in to the local paper."

"Wow. That's cool. You're out gathering material then?"

"Yup." My attention was caught by a Lab and his owner playing tug of war on the other side of the sidewalk. The Lab was winning.

"Where at?"

"Ruby Falls. I'm on my way back home."

"You'll have to tell me all about it this evening."

"This evening?" My mind went blank.

"We've got a date, remember?"

"Of course I remember," I lied. It was hard to concentrate on ordinary things like social engagements when you were ghost hunting.

"How do you like picnics?"

I hadn't been on a picnic since I was a kid. "It takes me back. I like picnics."

"There's a band contest in the park tonight. I thought we could take a picnic basket and listen to the local talent."

"Sounds like fun. When?"

"Six?"

"Sounds good."

"Are you comfortable with me picking you up?"

Second date, but the third evening I'd spent time with him. "Yes, I am." I rattled off the address.

"I'll see you at six."

I hung up and glanced at Liam, then pulled back onto the road, wondering what had brought that pensive expression to his face.

"Are you going to tell him about me?"

The question hung in the air between us.

"No, of course not. Why would you think that?"

"You told him you were writing a paper and that you'd tell him all about it tonight." His voice held a strained quality. He stared straight ahead.

"Liam, my dad always says if you have to lie, stick as close to the truth as possible. You'll be less likely to get tripped up."

"I like your father. He's a good man. He reminds me a bit of my da." Like a kid, he stuck his arm out the window to catch the wind.

"If I ever did write a piece on you, would you care?" I hadn't thought of it as a possibility till now.

He shrugged. "I don't know. It's one thing for your family and friends to know your history. It's another to be splashed across the front pages of a newspaper."

"Well I don't think getting on the front page need be a worry, but I get your drift." I swallowed my disappointment. Depending on the ending, it could have made a lovely story. And I was determined this story would have a happy ending.

"If it's important to you, girl, you know I'd never stand in your way. Why should it matter to me anyhow? It's not as if I'll be around to read it."

Not be around? My gut knotted. My hands clenched the steering wheel. The link between us was intensifying. How else did he know I now wanted to publish his story? I must not have done a good job of hiding my disappointment.

His expression was pensive, his eyes sad. As soon as he saw me watching him, he smiled. I swear the sun could take lessons from him on brightening a landscape. "So, we're going on a picnic. It will be nice being outdoors."

"Yes, it will." Grin. If Patrick only knew.

The phone rang again, and Liam moved it hastily out of my reach. "I'll see who it is." A young boy, riding on the passenger side of a sedan next to me in the passing lane, bobbed up and down in his seat as he pointed at the floating phone. The car sped by, the driver paying no attention. I gave a commiserating grin at the youngster twisting around in his seat, still pointing.

"That kid will be talking about the floating phone for weeks." A giggle erupted from my throat.

Liam didn't respond. The corners of his mouth drooped. Sadness permeated the car. "What's wrong?"

"I would have liked a family of my own, a son like that little boy, and a daughter."

"Oh, Liam." My heart tightened. "You'd have made a wonderful father. I trust when you reach the other side, you'll be so happy that you won't think about what you missed."

"I'm sure that will be the case." He glanced at the phone. "Your caller was Clayton. That one I won't miss. But I will miss you, lass."

I swallowed a lump in my throat. "I'll miss you too." I shook off my depression and tried for perky. It was harder than it should have been. "There's no need to worry about that yet, we still have plenty of time together. We've just started investigating."

"Right." He reached over and turned up the volume of the radio. Tunes blasted as we rode down the highway. We smiled at each other in perfect accord. Once the initial shock had worn off, Liam had developed a fondness for today's music. He had a good ear and a natural sense of rhythm. I deduced this by the way he stuck his head and shoulders through the top of the car and danced on the seat. And he thought my cell phone was a distraction when I drove.

By tacit agreement, neither of us talked anymore about Anna, William, or moving to the light. We both just wanted to pretend we were two young people enjoying each other's company. Who knew how much time we had left?

As we pulled in the drive, my cell rang again. I stifled a groan. "Hello, Clayton."

"Hi, Cat, how are you?"

"Fine, and you?" I turned off the motor and reached for the door handle. The car door swung open. With a flourish, Liam bowed and motioned me out. I lifted my hand as if I were royalty.

"Your highness." He bowed lower.

My nose in the air, I swept by him. As he caught up with me, laughter pushed up my throat and burbled over.

"What's so funny?"

I'd forgotten about Clayton. "Nothing."

"Do you always giggle about nothing?"

"What do you want?" Impatience had seeped into my voice.

"I thought I'd come over tonight."

"Sorry, I've got plans."

"What sort of plans?"

"That's really none of your business."

"Do you have a date?"

Irritated, I tightened my grip on the phone. "And if I do?" The soles of my sandals clipped against the sidewalk as I paced toward the door, and the spicy scent of azaleas that lined the sidewalk filled the air. A Monarch butterfly fluttered in front of me before it landed on a bush.

"Well, do you?"

If I said yes, maybe he'd stop calling. "Yes." I held my breath.

"Oh. Anyone I know?"

"That's none of your business," I repeated. "You know we're both free to see other people." The door opened of its own accord. I didn't know what I'd do when Liam moved on. I was so used to him opening doors for me I'd probably walk into them.

"Well that's right," he sputtered. "But I didn't realize you'd started seeing anyone since we began dating."

"Is this a problem for you?" I headed for the kitchen and a cold soda.

"You know I'd be perfectly happy for us to be exclusive if only you'd…"

"Put out," I suggested helpfully as I grabbed a soda.

"Well, I wouldn't have put it quite that bluntly, but yes. A man has needs."

Especially a young, horny one.

"I've got no problems with you seeing other women. You know that."

"Fine," he snapped. "I've got to go."

"Bye," I said into the dead phone. I popped the tab and took a deep gulp.

"Why are you still seeing him?" Liam had appeared at my elbow.

I thumped the can on the gleaming counter. "You've got to be going with someone to break up with them. Clayton and I aren't an item. We just occasionally keep each other company. But enough about Clayton. While

I get ready for my—er, our—date, I have a job for you." I headed for the bedroom, soda in hand.

He pulled out a pocket watch and snapped it open with his thumb. "It's only three o'clock."

"I need to decide what I'm going to wear, take a shower, fix my hair, put on fresh makeup, and a fresh coat of polish."

He shook his head.

"Never mind. Only another woman would understand." I splayed my fingers in front of my face. "I don't even know what color I want. Or what shoes to wear. Or…"

"What do you want me to do?" Liam interrupted, clutching his hair. "It's only a picnic," he muttered.

"Make a list of every guy you can think of who was interested in Anna." I pretended I hadn't heard the last comment.

He snorted. "That would be half the men in town."

"Then the sooner you get started, the better." I walked into the living room. "Marceee."

Silence answered. I backtracked to the dining room and found a note on the table that said not to expect her home till late.

The remote floated through the air. "I'll think better with the television on." We returned to the living room where he began surfing channels.

I stopped in my tracks and slapped my forehead.

"What's wrong?"

"When we were at the hotel, I should have asked to see the guest registry."

"I'm sure that's a great idea, but why in particular?" His gaze on the television, he sank into the couch and stretched out his legs.

Our link was such I was surprised he didn't figure it out immediately. "You said you got sucked up with some kind of Ghost Buster paraphernalia."

"Ghost Buster paraphernalia?" The look he sent me was less than complimentary.

"I should have checked the registry to see if Jonas Bromwell stayed in your room or Anna's." Back and forth. Back and forth. I strode in front of the sofa. Liam pulled in his legs so I wouldn't step on them. "I bet we'll find he stayed in one room, then made up some story to get in the other, like he'd forgotten his key. It may or may not help us figure out who your visiting spirit is, but it's another piece of the puzzle."

"Very clever deduction, but that comes as no surprise. You're an amazing woman, Caitlin." His glance lost its censure and his smile warmed me all the way to my toes. One minute he'd been sitting on the couch, the next he stood a breath away from me.

"And you're an amazing man-ghost." He was too. Even though he was nineteen and technically still a teenager, the term boy didn't apply to him. His features were rugged and his eyes held knowledge much older than any nineteen-year-old I knew.

We stared at each other while seconds ticked away. The physical tension between us felt like warm thick butter, and I forgot to breath. Desire stabbed me sharp and strong.

Liam cleared his throat and took a step back, clear across the room. "Well, I guess I better get on that list."

"Right. And I better polish my nails." I backed into the couch and sat down abruptly. He swept forward, reached out a hand to help me up, and then dropped it to his side. In his eyes burned the same longing that consumed me. He hurtled backward as I pushed off the couch and hurried to the bedroom. Once there, I shut the door and leaned against it, eyes closed, breathing heavy.

What am I doing? I can't be falling in love with a ghost.

Chapter 9

Shaken, I took a deep breath and decided a bubble bath would be good Zen. I lit candles and sank into water with bubbles to my chin. The tension in my shoulders and neck eased. I had a date with a charming young man. I would help Anna and Liam cross over to the other side. If my heart cracked a little in the process, it would heal. I was almost certain of it.

I soaked till my skin turned pruny and the water cooled. By the time I polished my nails with a coat of Fairy Wing Lilac and figured out what to wear, it was almost six. I'd changed a dozen times, finally deciding on a lavender and white striped shirt and jeans. I grabbed chunky amethyst earrings and headed for the living room just as the doorbell rang.

Before Liam could open it, I hurried to the door.

"You look sweeter than sugar, lass." He popped up at my elbow. I barely jumped. I was getting used to his appearing-disappearing act. "I like the little lavender straps on your feet. Sandals," he corrected himself.

"Thank you. Shoot, I don't have time to change to my lavender shoulder bag. Oh well, my tan canvas will have to do." Liam wisely said nothing, just shook his head.

I opened the door to find Patrick wearing a Duke T-shirt that had seen better days and scruffy jeans, frayed at the edges, with holes in the knees. One comprehensive look told me they hadn't come that way from the manufacturer. Why had I spent so long on my appearance? But the smile that lit up his face when he saw me made me decide maybe his clothes weren't so important after all.

"I know you hear this all the time but you are beautiful." He placed his hands on the doorjamb and just looked at me, his expression warm and appreciative.

"I feel overdressed," Liam commented, perusing Patrick much the same as I had a moment ago.

I bit my lips to keep from giggling. Would I be able to maintain a normal conversation with another person when there wasn't a running commentary from a ghost?

"If it looks like I didn't make an effort for you, I'm sorry. I had to work on a friend's car today and by the time I got it up and running, there wasn't time to throw my clothes in the laundry. This is all I had clean," Patrick explained.

"We're just going to the park anyway."

"Yeah, just pretend I've got on a better pair of jeans and a T-shirt without paint stains." He gave me his endearing quirky smile.

"Done." I walked out the door, relaxed and at ease with Patrick. "You're easy to be around and you're genuine."

"I try to be."

"A lot of my crowd isn't."

"Huh." He let the subject drop.

Of course, Patrick wasn't the only one who'd given me a different perspective on my values and that of my friends. Liam glided along on my other side, a look of disdain on his face. He was looking at Patrick's car, an older model compact. While not sexy, it was clean and looked to be in good condition. The ghost was becoming a car snob.

"I'd rather take your cousin's car," Liam sulked.

"You can't," I mumbled.

"Pardon me?" Patrick asked as he and Liam reached for my door.

"You can't imagine how I'm looking forward to the bands."

"Oof." Patrick apparently wasn't prepared for the ease with which his door swung open. I pretended not to notice as I slid inside the little car.

"It's got plenty of leg room," I pointed out to Liam as Patrick walked around to the other side.

"I'd still rather take Marcy's." He sat in the back, his arms crossed, his lips turned down.

"I just bet you would." Whether the male of the species was from the nineteenth or twenty-first century, when it came to boy toys, their response was the same.

"I'm sorry, did you say something?" Patrick folded his long frame into the car.

"I was just commenting on the leg room in your car."

"It has to have that." He laughed. "She's not pretty, but she's dependable, low maintenance, and high on fuel efficiency. If she were a woman, she'd be a cheap date."

Patrick dropped his hand from the key. He twisted in his seat to face me. "If that sounds like I'm a self-serving penny-pincher, I'm sorry. I try not to be self-serving. I do pinch pennies. I plan to go to medical school someday. It's not cheap." He quirked his lips and shrugged.

"Can your parents help you?" Paying for my education was a nonissue for me. To think about the kids who had to put themselves through school was humbling, especially when you were talking about years of education.

"They try, but my dad had a bout with cancer recently. They had to get into my college fund to pay the bills."

"I'm sorry." I reached over and grasped his hand. He flicked it over, palm up to clasp mine, his skin warm and vital.

Electricity jolted us. We jumped and dropped hands.

Liam's look was frosty. "I'm sorry for the lad, but you don't need to get all touchy-feely in front of me. It's not polite." He stared at me, unrepentant.

Touchy-feely? Liam had been watching too much TV.

"Wow, if touching your hand gives off sparks, I can't imagine what a kiss would be like." Patrick stared, his eyes wide, his hair on end.

A growl sounded from the back seat. Thunder boomed in a sharp crack directly over his side of the car. Patrick jumped, grabbed the steering wheel, and looked wildly around.

I cringed and closed my eyes. The chance of developing a love life with Liam around was slim to none.

"That was very weird." Patrick flexed his fingers before he started the car.

"Yes, wasn't it?" I responded, my voice as well as my throat dry. "Listen, Patrick, I hope you aren't looking for a relationship, my life's complicated right now," was the best I could come up with.

"I understand." He put his arm across the back of the seat and eased out of the drive.

"I doubt it." What an understatement.

"The other guy, right?"

You mean the other ghost?

"Clayton?" Liam and I said together. I rubbed my forehead where pressure built between my eyes. "No. Clayton and I aren't an item. What's your father do for a living?"

Patrick gave me a quick glance but took the hint. "My dad teaches history at the local community college and my mom's an admin assist at the same college."

"Really? That's pretty cool."

"Yeah, it is." His lips curved up in a smile that lit his whole face. "There was never a lot of money while I was growing up, but we never lacked for anything, especially in the things that counted. You?"

"My family's pretty tight too." I tried to include Liam in the conversation but his focus was elsewhere. My breath caught in my throat as he slid through the two-inch opening on the passenger window. What the heck was he doing?

"I need some air." He loped alongside the car, arms pumping, legs extended, looking around as he ran.

Who would have thought a ghost could move so fast? As one block turned into two and two into three with no mishaps, I relaxed. What trouble could he possibly get in? I shifted in my seat and chatted with Patrick.

Gliding alongside the passenger side of the moving car, Liam tapped on the window. Eyes bright with excitement, he pointed up the street at a shiny black sports car. He cut in front of Patrick's car to get a better look and slowed his pace.

Unfortunately, Patrick didn't. My heart rose in my throat as Patrick's car rolled straight through him.

Oh my God. Oh my God. I whipped around in my seat. Liam still stood in the middle of the road. I don't know who looked more astonished, me or the ghost. Luckily, Patrick was nearly at the park and paying attention to traffic.

Liam leaped to the car and slid in the back window. I opened my mouth to ask if he was all right, but my throat was too dry to say a word. It was just as well. By the disgusted look on his face, I gathered he was unharmed.

His next words confirmed it. "Lover boy needs to watch where he's going." Arms crossed, he glared at Patrick.

I didn't bother to point out the obvious, that Patrick couldn't see him. Even a ghost was entitled to be disgruntled after a car drives through him.

"We're here." Patrick flicked on the blinker and turned into the park. Adults, children, and dogs filled the recreation area. Blankets spread across the hillside like a crazy patchwork quilt. Patrick inched along behind a long line of cars, looking for a parking spot.

"This could take forever. I'm going to look for a place to park. Tell lover boy not to run over me." Liam disappeared through the roof of the car. Moments later, he was back. "Four cars up on the right. It's too tight for anything but a small car."

I took my cue, pressed my nose to the glass, and pointed. "Up there on the right."

"I don't see anything." Patrick hunched forward, squinting. He inched past a couple more cars. "I see it," he said, and flipped on his turn signal. "What, have you got x-ray vision?"

"Nope, a ghost whispered it in my ear."

Liam glared at me.

"Ha-ha. Good one." Patrick eased his car into the parking space and turned off the motor.

As we got out, a heavy metal band tuned up.

"This is going to be fun." Liam rubbed his hands together and eyed all the people strolling around the park.

"Yes, it is." His excitement contagious, I rose on my tiptoes trying to see the band.

"Excuse me?" Patrick had the trunk up. He pulled out a wicker basket, with a red and white checkered tablecloth folded over it, and a blue blanket.

"I said this is going to be fun." I borrowed Liam's phrase.

"It must be the music in the background, I could have sworn you said, 'yes it is.'" He shook his head.

He tossed the blanket over his shoulder and slipped his arm through mine. "Let's go find a place to sit."

For a moment, Liam's outline flickered with electricity. I stiffened. Then he shrugged. Apparently, he'd decided linking arms was not classified as touchy-feely.

The sun had gone down, leaving the sky a dull gray with a wisp of red where it met the earth. Stars began to twinkle. Soft grass tickled the sides of my feet, and the smell of hot dogs made my mouth water. Tension in my shoulders loosened as two young boys raced past us, then vanished altogether. "Thanks, Patrick, this was a great idea."

"I like the outdoors." He placed the blanket on the grass and lowered the picnic basket. "Do you like to hike?"

"My idea of hiking is trekking from one sale to the next."

Patrick laughed as he flipped a wrinkle out of the blanket.

"I do like to swim, though." I plopped down on the blanket. A thousand cushy blades of grass pricked through the cloth. Liam hovered beside me, his chin in his hand, his legs stretched out.

"Good for you." Patrick dug into the basket and pulled out a couple of bottles of water, biscuits, fried chicken, coleslaw, mashed potatoes, and brownies.

"I'm impressed." I reached for a bottle of water.

"I stopped at the local deli." He grinned, loaded up a plate, and handed it to me.

The band tuned up as the sky darkened. Fireflies blinked on and off as young children chased them.

"I'm going to stroll around." Liam floated to his feet and headed in the direction of the band.

I nodded and bit into my chicken.

Patrick gave me a quizzical look.

"What?" I said around a mouthful of food, my hand over my mouth.

"You do that a lot."

I swallowed. "Do what?"

"Nod, like you're carrying on a conversation I'm not aware of." He picked up a chicken leg and chewed thoughtfully.

"So I talk to myself. So what?" I jammed a forkful of mashed potatoes in my mouth. Maybe this wasn't going to be so much fun after all.

He reached over and touched my cheek with his finger. "It's not like you're talking to yourself. It's like you're talking to someone I can't see."

I choked. Patrick set down his plate and pounded me on the back. "Are you okay?"

"Fine," I whispered, in a hoarse voice.

"I didn't mean to upset you."

"You didn't."

Patrick continued to watch me, his features hard to read.

"You think I'm crazy." I put down my plate, my appetite gone.

"I think you're beautiful and mysterious. If you occasionally nod or shrug to yourself, you're entitled."

My insides warmed. Patrick was kind, caring, and fun. He made me feel good... When he wasn't commenting on me talking to myself.

"So are you excited about going to Virginia Tech this fall?" Patrick asked around a mouthful of coleslaw.

I nodded, then swallowed. We'd talked about schools last night. To both our delight we discovered we'd be at the same school. "I'll be rooming with Marcy. She'll be a sophomore this year."

Patrick set his plate aside and sprawled on the blanket belly side down, his lanky legs stretched out, his elbows propping up his shoulders. "Didn't you say you planned to major in journalism?"

"That's right."

"Journalism," he repeated, his forehead scrunched. "King!" He snapped his fingers. "Don King, Pulitzer prize winner."

"Um-hum."

"Your dad?" His eyebrows rose.

"Yup."

He whistled. "Wow. I'm impressed. His pieces on the oil spill and whale hunting were outstanding. Do you think I could meet him sometime?"

"Sure. Be warned, he'll talk your ear off. Dad loves nothing better than to pontificate on subjects near and dear to him."

Patrick grinned. "You must be very proud of him."

"I am." The band had switched out. The new group played blues. It wouldn't have been my first choice, but the lonely wail of a saxophone drifting on the air added a touch of romance to the evening. "Let me repeat, this was a great idea."

"Thank you." Head cocked to the side, he studied me.

"I wish you wouldn't do that." I shifted my position on the blanket.

"Do what?"

"Look at me like I'm a bug under a microscope."

"It's the biology major in me. Did I mention you're a very attractive bug?" he teased.

A laugh spilled out of my throat. "No one's ever said that to me before." I set my plate aside and stretched out on my stomach, my position mimicking Patrick's, our faces inches apart.

"I find you fascinating. If someone didn't take the time to get to know you, they'd fall for that ditzy demeanor you sometimes present, but underneath it is a very intelligent, warm young woman."

Still balanced on his elbows, he leaned forward and ran his thumb across my bottom lip, the touch as light and delicate as a surgeon's. My mouth opened, and my breathing became shallow. His lips touched mine.

Thunder exploded in the sky, and a white jagged lightning bolt struck next to the blanket.

We jumped back and stared at each other. Shrieks sounded in the background as a nearby baby cried. My eyes filled. This was so not funny.

"Did the earth move or was it just me?"

"In a manner of speaking."

Liam stood with his arms crossed, glaring at me.

"What are you staring at?" Patrick waved a hand in front of my face.

"Nothing," I whispered, my chest tight.

He looked at the sky. "Not to take anything away from our kiss, but I thought the heavens were about to open. But there's not a cloud or a drop of rain." He held his hand palm up.

I swallowed past my thickened throat. "Dry storm."

"Must be." Something in my voice caught his attention. He leaned forward and caught my chin to study my face. "What's wrong?"

I jerked my head away, afraid Liam might take exception. But Liam had disappeared. "Don't you find this"—I flapped my hand around—"a little odd?"

"All the electricity in the air when we touch?" He grinned at me.

"Yes."

"I find it a romantic coincidence. What else could it be?"

"Yeah, what else could it be?" I bit back hysterical laughter.

He leaned closer. "Shall we try again?"

I jumped back. "What could top thunder and lightning? I think I'll have another brownie." I scooted back and reached for a brownie, trying to ignore my tingling skin and racing heart.

"I don't want any complications right now," I mumbled indistinctly around a mouthful of decadent dessert.

"It was only a kiss, and a brief one at that."

With difficulty, I swallowed the large bite of gooey chocolate. "Kisses lead to complications."

"Is that the voice of experience talking?"

"Yeah." As of five seconds ago.

"No pressure then. When you decide you're ready for the complications, plant one on me. I'll cooperate fully." He wiggled his eyebrows.

"You're very special, Patrick." I started to cover his hand with mine, then thought better of it.

"Glad you noticed. And speaking of noticing, they've changed bands again."

We turned our attention to the stage. Gradually, I relaxed, but the shine had gone out of the evening. My preoccupation was such it took me a while to notice the growing buzz of the crowd. "There." "Look there." "How's that possible?"

I stood up and looked around. Liam carried a bunch of balloons. A balloon vendor ran behind him flapping his arms. At each child he came to, Liam handed out a balloon. It looked as though the balloons floated through the air to the children. A few parents thrust bills into the vendor's hands, thinking it was a magic act.

Laughing children followed the trail of balloons, squealing, "Me, me."

Liam continued to pass out the brightly colored, helium-filled rubber until only one remained. With children still trailing behind him, he walked to me. Children jumped in the air for the one remaining balloon that floated in the air. Solemnly, he handed it to me.

My hand reached out of its own accord, and our gazes locked for a long moment. Light shimmered up and down the string from his hand. The balloon glowed and expanded, while the crowd ooh'd and ah'd. With a loud pop, it burst, the pressure too great for the thin rubber casing. Liam disappeared as well.

The crowd that had followed the balloons slowly dispersed, chatting excitedly.

My limp legs gave. I dropped to the blanket, clutching the string and broken casing.

"Wow." Patrick plopped beside me. "I've got to tell you, I've never been on a date quite like this before. We touch hands and sparks fly, we kiss and thunder booms, and then a helium balloon floats right into your hand."

"Helium?" I still felt numb. It wasn't helium responsible for the balloon ending up in my hand. A certain ghost had placed it there, but I was perfectly happy for him to think it had floated there of its own accord.

"What else could it be? And those balloons going to the children... awesome. I'd love to know how the vendor did it."

I could tell him, but I wasn't about to. I put a shaky hand to my forehead. Liam hadn't hurt anyone. He was capable of it, but he hadn't hurt anyone. I repeated it to myself like a mantra.

I sat through the rest of the concert like a zombie, nodding occasionally at the—I hoped—appropriate moments when Patrick spoke.

When the last band began tuning up, we scooted out. Liam, who'd been conspicuously absent, met us at the car. The ghost slid into the back seat, his arms crossed, his head turned toward the side window.

As we drove home, Patrick critiqued the bands and marveled on the unusual events of the evening, still carrying the conversational ball. I added an occasional 'uh-huh.' When he pulled in the drive, I leaped out. "You don't have to see me in. Thanks, I had fun." Until a certain ghost stuck his nose in.

"I did too. I'll call you or you can call, especially if you want to put the moves on me."

Liam rumbled beside me. Then he disappeared...again.

Uneasy, I stepped away from the car. It began to roll backward out of the drive.

"Whoa." Patrick grabbed the wheel.

Even though I knew it was useless, I yelled, "Hit the brake!"

"I am!"

The car continued out into the street where it rolled to a stop. Thank God, there weren't any other cars around.

Patrick tried to turn it back into the driveway but it wouldn't turn. Instead, the car started moving down the street away from me and the house.

My heart pounding, I raced to the end of the drive, but the car was out of sight. "This is so not funny." I bit my lips, my hands clenched at my side. I paced back and forth on the sidewalk, lightheaded and overheated.

Finally, Liam appeared.

I shifted toward him and made an abrupt gesture with my finger. "You, to the back." I strode to the pool area, which I was starting to think of as our place.

Liam glided beside me, his arms across his chest, his look less than cordial. "He's fine. Just trying to figure out how his car turned into Herbie the Love Bug."

"Saw that on television, huh?"

Liam shrugged.

"You've got to stop this. You're ruining my life." I pressed my knotted stomach, hoping acid would quit spurting out of it.

The pool lights shone on his face. His features sharpened and became clearer. For a moment, he looked stricken. Then he went on the defensive. "Ye've no business kissing someone ye aren't betrothed to." He floated a foot above the ground, his expression self-righteous.

"We've had this discussion before; times are different now." I clutched my head and nearly howled.

"You're right, of course. I apologize." His voice sounded stiff and formal, his chin set at a pugnacious angle.

"Liam, I know this isn't a walk in the park for you, but our joined-at-the-hips routine is playing havoc with my social life."

He turned away from me and looked at the pool, his hands folded behind his back. I admired the long clean lines of him and, for a moment, wished... What was the use?

"Do you like him then?"

"Hm?" I was still caught up in the unearthly beauty of him.

He turned around but didn't look at me, his voice low. "Do you like him?"

"Do you mean like him, or like-like him?"

"Either. Both." He shrugged in an offhand manner, but hunched his shoulders as if against a blow.

"I like him. Do I like-like him? The potential is there."

Pain flitted across his face but was quickly masked.

My heart tightened.

"Then, I'll try to be more tolerant, but leave the sparking till after I've moved on to the next plane. Would you?"

"Deal."

He nodded and floated to the center of the pool.

"Liam."

"Yes?" He floated back toward me, the pool light haloing him.

"If you were human, I'd be way past the like-like stage with you."

He gave me a blinding smile. Oh my. My pulse jackhammered and my knees went weak. I bumped back against the chaise lounge and sat down.

"Lass, you're human and I'm a ghost, and I'm already way past the like-like stage. If I were human, I'd ask you to marry me."

My eyes filled, then ran over. Hot tears coursed down my cheeks and plopped on the chaise.

"Here now," he said alarmed. "I didn't mean to upset you."

I swiped at my eyes, then whispered, "If you were human and asked, I'd say yes," and knew it to be true. I'd always laughed at stories about star-crossed lovers. I never would again.

He looked at me with profound sadness.

What were we going to do? My heart constricted, painfully. Finally, I managed to shake off my despondency and ask, "Do you think that's where you're headed?" I pointed upward where a fat moon floated across the heavens.

He eased down on the chaise lounge next to mine and studied the moon. "I don't know. I don't know if there's a heaven or if we keep coming back to Earth till we get it right. I just don't know."

"If you came back, would you find me?" I continued to study the stars, unable to look at him for fear he'd read the longing in my eyes.

"If I came back, nothing would keep us apart."

His words warmed me, like a warm fire on a cold night. My ghost.

"But whether I move forward or come again, we need to find a way for Anna, William, and me to take the next step. I won't be the cause of your unhappiness."

"Your leaving won't make me happy."

"Nor me, but at least it won't draw out the pain."

My cracked heart cracked a little further. I rubbed at the ache.

Chapter 10

We were still sitting by the pool, both quietly absorbed in our confessions, when Liam announced, "I put together that list of boys interested in Anna." He drifted up and away from me.

"Oh good." My voice lacked enthusiasm. "What do you have?"

"Well, there's Jimmy Joe Davis, Johnny William Smith, Billy Bob Cook, Harley Snow…." He continued the list till I threw up my hands in surrender somewhere between Jackson Fansler and Homer Newton.

"How many?"

"Twenty-five, well twenty-six if you count Jacob, but he was only thirteen."

"Twenty-six?" Hammer-like blows throbbed at the base of my skull. "Can we eliminate any of them?" I stood. Caffeine would help my headache.

"How?" He trailed beside me as I headed for the house. The lights were out so I doubted if Marcy was home yet. From the movies, she'd probably gone to a party or spent the night with a friend.

"Did any of them marry while you were still alive, have children?"

"Good point." He gave me an admiring look. "Homer, Jacob—"

"Just give me a total," I interrupted ruthlessly.

He counted on his fingers. "That narrows it down to about twelve."

"Your sister was very popular." I flicked at a crumb on my shirt as I walked in.

"Everyone loved Anna," he said simply. "What do we do with the remaining twelve?"

"Online research. I may have to purchase some genealogy software." I headed for the kitchen, grabbed a soda, and guzzled. As the icy caffeine slid down my throat I could feel the tight band around my head loosen.

"What will that do?"

Sandra Cox

"It's just a way to narrow things down. Help us trace the ancestry of the twelve men interested in Anna. See if they married, had families. You know, there's nothing saying our specter couldn't be someone from her past with a dozen children, but I believe it's more likely to be someone that stayed single and pined."

"It's a wonderful idea, lass." His voice filled with enthusiasm and his dark eyes sparkled. His appearance grew brighter, more defined. I itched to touch his sharp cheekbones, push back the tumbled lock of hair on his forehead, run my finger over his appealing lips. Instead, I gave myself a brisk mental shake. "Good. Let's get started." I picked up my soda and headed for the bedroom and my little office.

"Now?" Liam looked surprised.

"Sure, why not?"

"No reason I can think of. What are we going to do?"

"We're going to make a list of those twelve or so people, put them in the computer, and see what we come up with."

I opened the door to my little office alongside my bedroom. Liam glided through the wall. I turned to the left, he to his right, and we collided. An electric shock picked me off the floor and arced me through the air. I landed on my butt. "Oof." Thank goodness for carpeting.

"Caitlin! Are you all right?" He was beside me before I hit the floor. He hovered nearby, wringing his hands, but not touching me. Dazed, I looked around and nodded. The hair on my arms stood straight up. I didn't want to even think about the hair on my head. A tingle still sizzled through me, along with a buzzing in my ears.

"Lass, are you hurt?" He squatted beside me, his beautiful eyes anxious.

I shook my head. My hair didn't move. It still crackled with electricity. I touched my arms. They were beginning to cool. Hopefully, my hair soon would too.

"Caitlin?" He leaned in.

"I'm okay." I pushed cautiously to my feet, thankful I wasn't a toasted marshmallow.

The ghost heaved a sigh of relief. His chest rose and fell through his old-fashioned clothes. He began to pace the room. "This is intolerable," he burst out.

"It was an accident." I reached out my hand before dropping it hastily as I realized what I'd started to do.

Liam's jaw set. "I have got to get to the other side. I will not hurt you. Help me. Promise me, you'll help me." He leaned toward me, eyes glowing feverishly.

"Promise," he repeated.

Even though it would break my heart to lose my ghost, I knew it had to be done. "I promise. Together, you and I will find a way to vanquish the evil spirit that is standing between Anna and your best friend and get all three of you to the other side." I spoke quietly, putting as much conviction as I possibly could into the words.

He studied my face for several seconds. Whatever he saw must have reassured him. "Together then, we'll follow our quest." Sadness lurked behind his smile.

"Let's do this thing." I took a deep breath and straightened my shoulders. "We'll start on the search."

"No, not tonight. You need to rest. I nearly fricasseed you." He grimaced.

"Actually, I feel just fine." It was true. "Maybe a good jolt occasionally clears the brain and gets the body going," I joked.

"It could have stopped your heart." He looked both fierce and stricken.

"But it didn't." I didn't bother to tell him my heart had stopped the first moment he appeared, and would never be the same again. "Now let's see what we can find out, shall we?" I settled at the computer and pulled up the Internet.

"What are you doing?" Liam approached and looked over my shoulder, staying well back.

I twitched my nose like a cat and breathed in cinnamon and limes. "You smell so good." I hadn't realized I'd spoken out loud until he responded.

"You smell lovely yourself, lass."

"Did everyone in your era say lass?" My nails clicked against the keyboard as I tried different names.

"Not everyone. My da used it quite a bit. Does it bother you?"

"No, I like it. Let's try this site." The directions were in small print at the bottom of the screen. It wasn't free, but I could navigate in it. "I think this one is going to work."

"Will this site show you what you're looking for?" He shifted on his feet and hunched his shoulders, leaning a bit closer to get a better look.

"Hopefully." I shifted to the side. My hair, which was still on end, touched Liam's shoulder. For a moment, the long strands glowed. "Wow. Guess there's some residual electricity left in my body."

Liam blinked, shook his head, and stepped back. "Sorry," he muttered.

"I'm fine, really. Got to get my credit card." I pushed up from my chair, tentatively touching my glinting strands. They crackled with electricity.

"What for?"

"To pay for the software." I trotted to the bedroom to get my plastic out of my purse, then entered the information and downloaded the software.

"It's not right." Liam rumbled over my shoulder.

"What's not right?" My attention fixed on the screen.

"You shouldn't have to pay to help me."

"Don't worry. It was a deal at thirty-nine ninety-five." I made a dismissive gesture with my hand. "Now give me the first name on your list."

"Jimmy Joe Davis." Liam floated to the front of the computer. He put his hands on his hips and rocked back on his heels.

"Jimmy Joe Davis." I typed it in.

Information scrolled across the screen.

"Great, there's twelve Jimmy Joe Davises." I groaned.

Liam moved behind me where he could read the screen. "But only two in Virginia and only one from Ruby Falls."

"Right." I tapped on the Jimmy Joe from Ruby Falls. We read the information together. "Looks like Jimmy Joe lived to the ripe ole age of eighty."

"And had six children and a passel of grand and great grandchildren," Liam added near my ear.

Once again, I breathed in cinnamon and limes. Heavenly.

"I don't think he's our boy." Liam stared at the screen.

"He did seem on excellent terms with his wife," I agreed. "Let's scratch him off our list." I pulled out a stenographer's pad and a gel pen, wrote out his name, and drew a line threw it. A thought struck me. "Can you write?"

"I can touch the TV remote, bring you a cup of coffee, and hold your cell phone. I would think so."

"Yeah, but writing leaves an actual physical imprint. Something left behind. You know what I mean?"

"I do, lass. Let's find out, shall we?"

I set the pen and pad on the desk beside the computer, then sucked in my breath as Liam picked up the pen and began making a list of the names we planned to check in a beautiful, old-fashioned scrawl.

"Wow." The breath I'd been holding whooshed out.

His eyes sparkled and he gave me an impudent wink. "This is much better than a quill and ink."

"No doubt." The pen gliding across the paper fascinated me. "Who's next?"

"Homer Newton."

"I can't believe we'll have to look through too many Homer Newton's."
I typed it in. Sure enough, only one Homer Newton popped up.

"Homer became a priest?" Shock filled Liam's voice as he read the information the computer spewed out.

"I take it that surprises you."

"There was no bigger hell raiser in the county than Homer Newton."
He shook his head and drew a line through Homer's name.

"Next."

"Johnny William Smith."

The computer spit out line after line of Johnny William Smiths. "This will take forever," I wailed.

"Can you limit it to Virginia?"

"I did."

"Can you limit it to the 1800s?"

"I did."

* * * *

Sunshine filtered in from the partially closed blinds. I put the pillow over my head and drifted back to sleep.

A scream woke me.

I bolted upright, stubbed my toe jumping out of bed, and hopped into the living room on one foot, holding the other.

Marcy stood in the middle of the living room, shrieking.

"What is it?" Goose bumps roughened my skin. My breath whistled in and out in short sharp pants.

She pointed at the cup of coffee sitting sedately on the mahogany table in front of the couch.

"What?" Still not completely awake, I frowned in bewilderment at the cup. My gaze lit on Liam standing nearby.

I picked it up and gulped, nearly purring in ecstasy. As the caffeine kicked in, the fog around my brain lifted. With it came the horror of understanding. "You didn't," I mouthed.

"I was bringing you coffee," Liam said with injured dignity.

"The cup floated through the room, just like the gravy boat," Marcy shrieked. She sank down on the couch, hair falling forward as she put her head in her hands. "I'm having a breakdown."

"I'm going to have to tell her." I swallowed a sigh.

"Who are you talking to? There's no one there. Are you having a breakdown too?" Momentarily diverted, Marcy lifted her head.

I sank down on the couch beside my cousin. "Marcy, can you keep a secret?"

"How can I know? I've lost my mind."

"Of course you haven't," I soothed. "Remember your ghosts?"

"That was all a hoax." She sniffed and blew her nose. "Did I tell you, Bromwell sent me a check?"

"No, did he?" What were the ethics on that since technically half the goods Marcy bought hovered near the ceiling?

My cousin nodded, twisting the rings on her finger.

"Let me get you a cup of coffee."

"Don't mention coffee." She shuddered.

I gathered my courage. "Prepare yourself."

That got her attention. She pulled herself together and looked at me warily. "What?"

"There were ghosts in the vials." Whew. There, I'd said it.

"What are you talking about?"

"One of the ghosts escaped before it got here, but Liam didn't." The words tumbled out on top of each other.

"Liam?" She gave me an uneasy look.

"Liam O'Reilly."

Liam stood and bowed.

"I don't see anyone."

"I know. I'm the only one who can see him."

"What? But I paid for him. Why can't I see him?" Marcy's hysterics had dried up, her curiosity aroused.

"I don't know."

"How do you know he's here?" She looked around her.

"I can see him, hear him."

"So you're saying you can see and hear him, and I can't." She tapped her crossed forearms with her perfectly manicured French nails, a skeptical look on her face.

Couldn't say I blamed her for that. "Well, yeah."

"Honestly, Caitlin, is this some kind of bid for attention? I'm sure the ghost is here." She waved her arm dramatically. "But I don't believe for one moment you can see and hear him and I can't."

Uh-oh, Marcy was normally the soul of amiability.

She snapped her fingers. "I get it. You've just gone into character for your play."

"That's right." Inside I was yelling whoopee and doing handsprings. It was so unfair of me not to want to share Liam with my cousin, but at least I'd tried.

Liam's head swiveled back and forth between us like a spectator at a tennis match.

"So you think it's the ghost?"

"Of course, what else could it be? And don't go calling him Liam. I'll name him." She fingered her chin. "How about Edward?"

I bit my lips together but couldn't repress the giggle. I looked over at Liam.

He stood with legs akimbo, arms crossed, and a frown on his forehead. "Edward?" He rolled his eyes.

When I didn't respond, she glanced at me. "What's wrong with Edward?"

I tried for diplomacy. "Nothing, but maybe we should wait until we find out what his name really is."

"Then why were you calling him Liam?"

"In character."

"I still can't believe you're trying out for a play. Oh by the way, your dad picked up his car and dropped off yours."

"My car's fixed?" My insides quivered, all thoughts of naming the ghost forgotten.

"Yup."

"Yes. Yes. Yes. Yes, yes, yes, yes." I did a happy dance.

Liam drifted through the wall and outside. I grabbed the cup of coffee and took a quick glug before I raced to my room, threw on shorts and an old tie-dyed T-shirt, and followed him out.

The ghost stood staring at my car. "It's not a Corvette." Disappointment laced his voice. "It's round and it's little and it's...pink."

"It's a bug." I adored my car. "When I wrecked it, Dad threatened to get me something large and sturdy, but I pleaded till he caved."

"No, it's a car.... And it's pink. And your dad was right about the large and sturdy, unless he intended to buy you a Corvette."

"They're called bugs. And I don't know why you keep nattering on about its color. Dad and Mom ordered it for my birthday. It's one of a kind." Pride rippled through me.

"I can see why it's called a bug, and I keep on 'nattering' as you call it because it's a girl's car. What self-respecting man would drive a pink car?"

"It's fun. You'll like it." I danced around my little bug, giving it love pats. "Come on, I'll take you for a spin." I had the car door open and my hind-end hoisted in the air before it dawned on me I didn't have any makeup on. I head slapped myself. "What am I thinking? I haven't

showered, no makeup, my hair's a mess. It must be all the stress...
Edward." I grabbed my stomach and giggled.

"Ha-ha."

I'd started toward the house when a thought stopped me in my tracks.
"I hope Marcy doesn't decide to hold a séance."

"Lor' save us. Though it might be entertaining." He rubbed his chin
with his thumb and forefinger. The bright sun shone straight through him.

"Do you think the creepy specter would appear?" An idea was forming
in the back of my brain, but whether good or bad I had no idea.

"I hope not. Whoever he is, he's been quiet lately. I'd like to keep it
that way."

"Can't argue with you there. We've narrowed our list down to seven
possibilities. What say we go back to Ruby Falls today? We can see how
Pinkie handles after her time in the shop. We might run across something
in the Preservation Library we've missed."

As we trotted up the walk, he picked a pink azalea off a nearby
bush and placed it in my hair. The gesture bemused me. A light electric
current pulsed through me and with it, sanity. "Liam, you can't just go
around carrying coffee cups in midair and putting flowers in my hair."
Nerves skittered up my spine and climbed my neck. "What if someone's
watching?"

"Sorry, lass. It just seems the most natural thing in the world to do,
as would kissing you." He stared into my eyes. His outline grew more
pronounced, as it did when his emotions were near the surface.

My lips parted. Our gazes locked. His wonderful scent filled my senses,
and the tension in the air thickened. Without thought, I leaned forward.

He took a quick step back. "The sooner we find what's keeping William
and you know who apart, the better, for both of us." The pain that pierced
my heart was reflected in his eyes. He straightened and cleared his throat.
"You need your coffee. It will make you feel better."

"No doubt." My lips quivered. I forced them up in a shaky smile.

We strolled up the walk in silence. As he reached for the door, I put my
hand on it for form's sake. Marcy turned from the living room window.

Oh great.

"Practicing your lines?"

"Yeah." Since she wasn't having hysterics, I cleverly deduced she
hadn't seen the floating flower. I hated lying to Marcy, but I couldn't bear
to share Liam. I'd share anything else, but not my ghost. Our relationship
was too personal, too private.

"When are tryouts?"

"In a couple of weeks. Are you interested?" I was safe on that one. Marcy had no interest in acting.

"No, but I might consider working behind the scenes. Maybe help with the design."

"That would be nice." Now what did I do?

"Do you think we should have a séance?"

I knew it.

I headed straight for the coffeepot, poured a cup of the steaming brew, and loaded it down with sugar and cream. After I'd drunk half a cup, my coping mechanism kicked in.

"I don't know. Do you know any mediums?"

"No." Regretful, she shook her head, then snapped her fingers. "Ouija board."

It seemed the lesser of two evils. "That's a thought."

"Pour me a cup, would you?"

Luckily, Liam had made coffee in the regular pot instead of the single pod server. I reached into the cabinet and pulled out Marcy's Shop Till You Drop mug, decorated with pink stilettos, and filled it up.

"Thanks. Sorry, if I snapped at you. I know you were just in character for the play when you said you could see my ghost. But seeing that floating cup was pretty unnerving." She reached for the sugar bowl and liberally doctored her coffee.

"I'm sure it was," I soothed, mentally grinding my teeth over the "my ghost" remark.

"And I'm feeling rather guilty about insisting Bromwell return my money."

"Don't. He had no business trying to sell ghosts in the first place. It's like selling slaves."

"Good point." She sipped delicately before setting her cup down. "I'm going shopping with Melinda, and then we're getting pedicures. Want to come?"

I loved pedicures. I wiggled my bare toes and imagined them in hot, foaming water. But I had to take one for the team. "No, I think I'll just hang. Maybe I'll try to hook up with my parents. Buy them lunch to thank them for the use of their car and picking up Pinkie." I crossed my fingers behind my back. I'd said maybe, not definitely. "But thanks anyway."

"Okay. Well, I'm going to take a quick shower before I pick up Melinda." Marcy took another couple sips of coffee and strolled out.

Once Marcy left, my tight muscles loosened, then tightened again when the coffee pot hovered over my cup followed by the sugar and creamer. "Don't do that!"

His expression turned hurt. "I like to do things for you."

"Don't do that either," I whispered.

"Don't do what?" He arched his eyebrows, confusion on his features.

"Give me that hurt look that melts my resolve and cracks my heart."

The mischievous, lopsided grin I loved was back in place. "Here now, we can't have your heart cracked." He handed me the cup of coffee.

I buried my face in it and sipped. "Perfect."

"Let's take a look at our remaining ghostly suspects before I get cleaned up." I pushed back from the counter.

"Sure."

Cup in hand, I meandered to the bedroom and my office closet. Liam didn't bother with the door, just passed through the wall as usual.

I slid into the chair, picked up the list, and read the first name. "What do we know about Bobby Johnson?"

Liam picked up a sheet of paper we'd made notes on. Some information was from the Internet, some from what he remembered. "Bobby was two years older than Anna, never married, had a crush on her in his teens but wasn't seen after the war." Liam paced back and forth, his hands locked behind his back.

"Johnny William Smith." I read the second name.

"Johnny William was the same age as Anna. He got angry when she wouldn't go out with him."

I looked at Liam and arched my eyebrows.

He continued, "Got a girl pregnant shortly after that and married her. She died in childbirth, no record of him ever marrying again."

"I don't think I like Johnny William Smith. We'll leave him on the list." I took a sip of coffee. Cold. I grimaced and set the cup down.

"He was a bit of a bully," Liam confirmed, as he rocked on his heels, his fingers splayed low on his waist.

"Next, Ezekiel Daniels."

"We're not alone," Liam muttered near my ear and slid the paper he held onto the desk.

"Cat, can I borrow your green sandals?" Marcy peered over my shoulder. The light floral fragrance she wore drifted around me. "What are you doing?"

I pressed my lips together and forced myself not to give a guilty start. "Just trying to get in character." I waved the sheet of suspects. "There're all kinds of bad boy ghosts."

"Hey!" Before I knew what she meant to do, Marcy grabbed the sheet of paper out of my hands.

"Who wrote these names? This definitely isn't your handwriting. It looks like something from another century."

My mind went blank.

"Someone else trying to get in character," Liam improvised.

"It came with the script. No doubt, someone else is trying to get in character," I parroted.

"Oh." She lost interest and laid the list back on the desk. "Can I borrow the sandals?" She wore an olive, pleated pullover with khaki cuffed shorts and a jade bracelet.

"Of course, they'll go perfectly with your outfit. You look like a million."

"Thanks, see you this evening." She blew me a kiss and disappeared through the door.

"I better get ready too." I pushed back the chair and stood up. "Get lost."

"I'll go watch TV." His face took on a look of pleasure.

"Just wait till Marcy's gone."

"Of course."

"Um-hmm," I said skeptically as he disappeared through the wall.

Chapter 11

"You look pretty as a picture." His lips tilted up, and his eyes warmed with admiration.

"Why thank you." I wore a pink scoop neck tee with white slacks, and pink leather and cork sandals. It had taken all the ingenuity in my limited repertoire of BS to convince him riding in a pink car would not lessen his manliness. Men.

"What's that?" He pointed to the back seat.

"My tablet. Aileen pointed out that I hadn't brought a notepad. This is like a miniature computer," I explained. "Go ahead and check it out."

It floated through the air. He spent the next several minutes playing with my toy. "Do you have any games loaded on it?" He scrolled the screen.

"We'll download some later. You figured the one's out on my computer pretty quickly," I commented. Liam grunted, his eyes on the screen.

"So how do you like Pinkie?"

"It's got plenty of leg room," he said diplomatically.

"It does, doesn't it?" I agreed.

"And it suits you."

"You think so?" A rush of pleasure shot through me.

"Yes. Not that you don't look hot driving a Corvette."

I laughed. "With all the television you've been watching, your language is a blend of the old and new. It suits you."

From there we segued into a conversation of colloquialisms. Liam and I could talk for hours on any subject. Since he'd burst into my life, every day had been an adventure. Before I knew it, we'd arrived at the Ruby Falls exit.

"Where do you want to go first, the hotel, the Preservation Library or the Hall of Records?"

"The hotel." The lilt died from his voice.

"You want to see Anna."

"For all the good it will do me."

"Hey." I reached over to touch him, then dropped my hand. "You and Anna and—" I stopped as Liam gave me a warning look. The spirit had been quiet lately. As long as I didn't link William's and Anna's names, he didn't bother us. "Well anyway, it won't be long till you've moved into the light. I've got to tell you I don't think our malignant friend is overly bright. The only thing that sets him off is—"

Liam cleared his throat.

"Right."

A few minutes later, we pulled into the hotel. When we walked in, an elderly couple was just checking out. While Aileen's head was bent over the bill, I whispered out of the corner of my mouth, "I'll hang out with Aileen if you want to go check on Anna."

"All right." He disappeared. One moment he stood beside me, the next he was gone.

Aileen looked up. Her face lit up when she saw me, and she came around the reception desk to greet me. "Hello, dear."

"Hi, Aileen." I held up my tablet. "I brought something to take notes on this time."

"Ooh, I want one of those. Can I see it?"

Amusement tickling my throat, I handed it to her.

She slid smoothly from one page to another with her index finger. "Want some coffee?" Her head down, she continued to scroll.

She went to the bookstore and headed for the erotic section. She glanced up and caught my shocked stare.

"I may be old but I'm not dead." She winked, closed out the site, and handed me back my tablet. As we strolled into the room behind the reception desk she asked, "Have you discovered anything since you were last here?"

"Yes and no."

"Spoken like a politician." She paused as she reached for the coffeepot. "Would you rather have iced tea?"

"That sounds good."

Ice cubes crackled as she pulled a tray out and twisted it. She poured tea out of a plastic container with an orange lid and handed it to me. The tea was so sweet I could feel cavities form. "Just the way I like it. This is great. Thanks."

"So what have you discovered, dear?" She sank into the portable secretary's chair, crossed her legs, and smoothed out her black slacks.

"I went online and did a search of young men who would have been the same age as…"

"Anna O'Reilly?"

My iced tea went down the wrong way and I choked.

"Are you all right, dear?" She got up and patted me lightly on the back, then sat back down. "Now what were you saying?"

I cleared my throat. "I went online and did a search of young men who would have been Anna's age and crossed off those who'd married and begat children." Begat? I sounded like a genealogy tract.

"Mm-hmm." Aileen nodded vigorously.

"If they had children and grandchildren, I scratched them off my list, as having no time to pine after Anna."

"That's good," she enthused.

"I've got about seven names left that I'm going to research. By the way, I didn't realize you actually knew the names of the ghosts."

"My great granny talked about it. Her momma knew the family when she was a little girl. Terrible tragedy. Died on her wedding day. Now if you were to ask most folks in town, they'd know the legend but not the names. That's about died out, but you're going to rectify that, aren't you?"

"I'm certainly going to try. And speaking of it, I'd better get to the Preservation Library. I'd like to take a look at the pictures, then go to the Hall of Records and check on those names." I pushed to my feet.

"Do you have the list with you, dear? I might be able to help."

"Yes, I do." I dug the list out of my handbag.

"What a darling purse," she said admiringly. "I love pink and black. Don't you? And that darling little pink cloth flower just sets it off."

"Thanks." I adored Aileen and hoped I was half as peppy when I got to be her age.

She pushed her modish black frames up on her nose with her index finger and unfolded the list. "I think you can rule out Tommy Jones."

"Why is that?"

"He was the skeleton in the family closet." She leaned closer. "Gay."

My eyes widened. "How do you know that? Never mind, your momma right?"

She nodded. "Small Southern towns."

"Thanks, that will save me some time."

She studied the list again and gave me a speculative look. "You have quite remarkable penmanship for one of your generation."

"Calligraphy," I lied.

"Well, it's the best I've seen in many a year."

She handed the paper back to me. I took out a purple gel pen and crossed through Tommy Jones's name. I wondered if Liam knew about Tommy.

"Thanks, Aileen, you've been very helpful." I held out my hand. She ignored it, put her arms around me, and gave me a feathery kiss on the cheek. The strong scent of incense enveloped me. My nose tickled, and I tried not to sneeze.

"My pleasure, my dear. It's just so exciting having our story told. I can't wait for the book to be published."

"Well, I may not get a publisher to buy it." I prevaricated, feeling guilty about leading this delightful little ole lady on.

"Nonsense, if you can't find a publisher with enough sense to buy your book, self-publish. It's all the rage these days."

"Good idea." The writer's genes I'd tried so hard to ignore stirred. I wanted to write this story, and I wanted to publish it.

We walked toward the lobby. Liam wasn't there. If he wasn't ready, I'd wait outside.

"Do you want to go upstairs and have another look around?" Aileen asked.

"No. Thank you, though." I couldn't bear to watch Liam's silent suffering. I was being a coward, but I couldn't stand to see him in pain. And if his twin ached, he ached right along with her.

Liam appeared as we neared the entryway, his outline more misty than normal, his color less clear. My heart caught in my throat. I forced my attention back to Aileen.

"I'll just ring up Ethel and let her know you're coming. If anyone can give you information on the star-crossed lovers, she can. Wait till I tell her you're trying to reunite—"

"Don't let her finish," Liam shouted.

I opened my mouth to interrupt her, but it was too late.

"Anna and her William."

A carved antique table with a clear, pretty vase of crimson peonies crashed to the floor. The vase exploded in a geyser of crystal. Red petals scattered among the broken prisms of glass like splotches of blood.

Chapter 12

"Oh, dear," Aileen said inadequately.

"Aileen!" A small trickle of blood coursed down her paper-thin cheek. Her blush stood out in garish contrast to her blanched complexion. "You're hurt!"

She touched her cheek and stared at the crimson drop on her finger in wonder. "It's nothing, just a scratch."

"We've got to get that seen to. Do you have a first aid kit? Where's your bathroom? You better sit down," I babbled, shaking like a leaf.

Liam circled us, his outline sharp and defined. The light of battle shone in his eyes. "Come on out and fight, you bloody bastard."

He was upset to be cursing. For some reason, it calmed me. I took Aileen by the shoulder. "Let's go to your bathroom and get you cleaned up before I deal with this mess."

"That's not necessary, child."

"I insist."

"If you'll sweep this up, I'll go clean my face." She looked around and shook her head. "I've got to quit putting my good vases on that table."

"Where's the broom?"

She pointed to a small door against the far wall.

I trotted over, opened the door, and pulled out a broom and dustpan. "Does this happen very often?"

Aileen stood, tapping her finger against her cheek as if in thought. She looked at me, and her eyes sparked with excitement. "You know I never made the connection before, but it only seems to happen when I mention Anna and—"

Before she could continue, I leaped forward and placed my hand over her mouth.

She nodded vigorously. I took my hand away.

"That must be the trigger. Our malignant spirit's trying to keep them apart." She all but danced around.

"That must be it. You're a regular sleuth." I pushed enthusiasm into my voice.

"How exciting." She clapped her hands together. "I better go wash my face. I'll be right back."

When she disappeared, I turned to Liam. "She could have been hurt. We've got to put a stop to this."

"We're going to," he said, his countenance grim, his legs akimbo.

"Right." I didn't mention I hoped no one else got hurt in the process.

As I emptied the shards of glass and blood-red peony petals into the wastebasket, Aileen walked back in carrying a roll of paper towels. I took the towels from her and began to sop up the puddle of water on the hardwood floor.

"Thank you, dear. I called Ethel; she's expecting you. It's the only other old building on the block. You'll recognize it."

"Thanks." The dripping towels gave a soft thump as I dumped them into the wastebasket. "I'll be in touch."

"Just a minute." She trotted to the backroom and came back carrying a plastic bag filled with cookies. "Something to snack on going home. I know how you young people get hungry."

"Thanks." The gesture touched me. "How's the cheek?" She'd cleaned it up. It was a thin scratch that ran from under her eye to her chin. On a young person, it would heal in a few days, but Aileen was no longer young.

"It's nothing." She made a dismissive gesture with her hand. "It'll be good for business. By this time tomorrow they'll probably be saying the ghost decapitated me." She laughed.

I didn't. "Don't even say such a thing." My stomach spurted acid. What a horrible thought. What was this spirit capable of?

"I was just teasing, dear. Our ghost has never hurt a soul. I just happened to get in the way."

"Well, whoever he is, I'm not letting him off the hook that easily. What if the shards had caught your eye?"

"I'm wearing glasses, dear. Now go talk to Ethel and see if you can solve this mystery and reunite the star-crossed lovers."

My stomach tightened. But the term star-crossed lovers didn't seem to have any effect on our malignant spirit. "Right." I gave her a quick hug, her bones as frail as a bird's beneath my hands, and left.

"Whew." As I closed the door, the bell tinkled behind me. Liam's features were sharp and defined. His fists still clenched.

"He could have hurt you," he said between his teeth as he floated to the car and opened the door.

I stood on the edge of the street lost in thought till a car honked and swerved. I slid in, and Liam banged Pinkie's door shut.

"What?" He slid in through the roof.

"The spirit has never tried to hurt us, just warn us off." I started the motor and pulled into traffic.

"He hurt a little old lady and he could have hurt you." There was a pronounced tic in Liam's jaw.

"But he didn't."

"This time."

"Pleasant thought," I muttered.

He continued, "There's a cold hazy barrier I can't break through. I can only catch glimpses of a dark outline."

"Can't make out who it is?"

"No."

"Well, we can scratch Tommy Jones off the list." I pulled to a stop in front of an old one-story building with the words Preservation Library painted in gold above the door. "He was gay. But you wouldn't know what that means."

His head swiveled toward mine like an exorcist victim, jaw dropped and eyes widened. "I know what it means. I watch the news. But Tommy Jones? You must be mistaken."

"It's okay to be gay in today's world."

"I know; I watch the news," he repeated and hunkered down in the seat, his face bright red. "How do you know that he was, was…"

"Gay?" I finished helpfully. "Aileen told me. Her great granny was told by her momma. Apparently, it was the town scandal."

"I don't doubt that." He shook his head. "You'd never know from the stories he told."

"I loathe sexual prowess lies. I doubt there's a girl in school that hasn't been the butt of one. Tell me you never bragged about that sort of thing."

"I would never betray a young woman who gifted me with her favors. I'm a gentleman." He lifted his chin and his eyebrows drew together.

"Of course you are. I should never have questioned it. Let's go in." My seatbelt snapped into its holster as I pushed the button and he opened the door. "Thanks. Did you speak to Anna?"

"If that's what you'd call it." His face lost its animation.

I wished I hadn't asked and refrained from any further questions as we entered the library. The door creaked when Liam opened it. I didn't even bother to put my hand on it and pretend. The smell of must and old books hit me in the face as we walked in, and I put a finger under my nose so I wouldn't sneeze.

A woman who made Aileen look like a teenager hobbled toward us, leaning heavily on a cane. I swear I could hear her bones creak.

"You must be Caitlin. Aileen called and said you were on your way. She also said there'd been paranormal activity." Her eyes glinted behind thick glasses. Where Aileen still dressed like a youngster, Ethel wore a long, shapeless paisley mauve dress with a starched lace collar and black thick-soled shoes.

"That's right. A flying vase. We appreciate you letting us— I mean, I appreciate you letting me look around."

She looked at me strangely. Not that I blamed her. With each passing day, Liam had become more real to me. It was as natural to be with him as it was to breathe. I no longer considered him ectoplasm, just Liam. Someone who'd become a part of my life.

"What a lovely shawl." I pointed at a black silk wrap with red cabbage roses on it, faded but still beautiful. I crossed my fingers and hoped it would distract her from my strange comment.

"It is, isn't it? The Baumgartner family donated it. It came all the way from Paris."

"It's very pretty." My pulse quickened. The wall to the right of the silk wrap was lined with old pictures. What were they called, daguerreotypes? Tintypes?

Ethel noticed my interest. "Feel free to look around. If you need me, I'll be at my desk." She hobbled to an antique desk and pulled out a book with a lurid cover. I choked on a snort. She and Aileen might not dress alike, but they were kindred spirits in their reading material.

I meandered around the room, studying the pictures. There were hundreds of them, with no rhyme or reason. In the later pictures, film had replaced plates. On the far wall, photos in color were creeping in. I ignored them and studied the older pictures.

"Caitlin."

Something about the timbre of Liam's voice had me hurrying to his side.

"What is it?"

"Did you say something, dear?" Ethel glanced up.

"I talk to myself. Sorry I bothered you." I really had to stop that.

She nodded and went back to her book.

If Liam noticed my gaff, he paid no attention, his focus on a six-and-a-half by eight-and-a-half picture in front of him.

"Oh, it's you and your family," I breathed. There could be no mistake. A beautiful woman sat beside a handsome man. Liam stood behind and to the side of their mother, and Anna behind and to the side of their father. Even with the stiff pose, I could see the twinkle in Liam's eyes. His twin looked just like him, only petite and feminine. Their eyes were shaped like their mother's and they had her dark hair, but the sensuous mouths belonged to their father.

There were three more: one of his parents, one of Anna, and one of Liam, his hand on his horse's neck. I lingered the longest on the photo of Liam. It reminded me of the night we'd driven to the ocean and he'd told me he loved to ride.

I had to have that picture. I dug into my purse, pulled out my phone, and snapped pictures. I took three of Liam with his horse to make sure I got at least one good one.

"Ahem."

My pulse jumped as Ethel cleared her throat. I'd been so engrossed I'd never noticed her approach.

"I hope you don't mind." I slipped my phone back in my purse.

"For the book?"

Ah, Aileen had been a busy bee. "Yes." And for my bedside table.

"Just be sure to mention they were taken at the library, dear."

"I will."

She hobbled off again, and I went back to studying the portraits.

There was one more picture taken in front of a little white church with a tall steeple. A group of people stood in front of it. The women held picnic baskets. I leaned closer to study it. Most stared at the camera, except Anna, who gazed up at a handsome young man, her face filled with adoration. "William?" I asked under my breath. Another boy stared at Anna.

Liam nodded, his gaze fixed on the picture.

"Who's that?"

"Who?"

"The young boy staring at your sister."

"Oh, that's Ezra Ames. He was always under foot. He wasn't quite right, but harmless."

I wonder...

"Amazing. You've done your homework. How did you recognize the star-crossed lovers? At least that's what Aileen and I think. Just look at the way she looks at him. Aileen promised not to tell. We wanted to see if you could pick them out." Ethel nodded her approval.

I didn't need to answer, just nod as she kept up a running commentary. She followed my involuntary glance to Liam's picture.

"The brother. Handsome as sin, wasn't he?"

"Oh yes."

Liam reddened, poofed to the other side of the room, and hung out near the ceiling.

"And quite the ladies' man if the legends are to be believed."

"Oh really?" Acid spurted in my tummy. I curled my toes to keep from tapping them. Geesh. Jealous of women from a bygone era. *Get over it, Caitlin.*

"But a good lad all in all."

She glanced at the picture taken at the church picnic, Anna and William in the front row. "I'm assuming that's her young man there, but I have no documentation to back it up."

"I think you're right." My heart melted as I gazed at the picture. Even given its age, you could still see the love for him in her eyes.

I would reunite them. That was a promise.

Determined, I turned to Ethel and held out my hand. "Thank you. You've been very helpful. I need to check records of births and deaths. I guess I'll try the courthouse."

"Try the vital statistics office at the town hall, dear. Ask for Mary, I'll let her know you're coming." Her thin fingers clasped mine in a surprisingly strong grip.

I said good-bye and made a dash for my car. The door opened a nanosecond before I got there.

"Thank you." I didn't bother to remind the ladies' man it was a bit over the top for a car door to open by itself. Opening doors for women was as natural to him as breathing.

We headed for the town hall. While not beautiful, the building had a quiet dignity about it not found in modern structures.

I parked, then pulled the list out of my pocket. "We're down to six: Bobby Johnson, Johnny William Smith, Ezekiel Daniels, Harley Snow, and Ulys Horntrop."

"What do you hope to find here?" Liam studied the building, his look pensive.

"I'm not sure, just hoping to narrow the list. Maybe a marriage that we weren't aware of, births, the same as before."

"Okay, let's go in."

We walked in the door and looked at the listing of agencies and room numbers. I studied it till I found Vital Statistics. "One floor up."

We took the stairs, then turned left. On the right, Vital Statistics was painted on the glass door.

A bell tinkled as I pushed through. A young woman, who didn't look much older than me, spoke around a mouthful of gum. "May I help you?"

"I'm looking for Mary." I approached the counter.

"That would be me." She popped her gum.

"Oh, hello." Up until now, the women I'd met had been on the other side of seventy.

"You must be Caitlin." She studied me with open interest.

"That's right."

"What records would you like to see?"

I pulled out my list of names and handed it to her.

"Keep in mind Ruby Falls didn't start keeping records till 1878." She blew a large bubble.

"Oh." My tummy turned over.

"I could probably help you with Ezekiel Daniels." Mary leaned on the counter and studied the list.

"Really?"

"Yes, he was my great, great, great uncle and a Baptist minister."

Liam shook his head in disbelief. "Who'd have thought Ezekiel would become a man of the cloth."

"You don't say. I'm assuming he married."

"Actually, no."

"No?" A chill crawled down my spine.

"It was such a sad story. He'd fallen in love later in life. They were going to be married, but she caught scarlet fever and died."

The air went out of my lungs in a whoosh. Well, that let Ezekiel off the hook. "How sad."

"It is, isn't it, and terribly romantic." She studied the list. "The handwriting is amazing."

"Calligraphy."

"Cool. I've been thinking about trying it. Just have a seat, this may take a while."

My sandals clip-clopping, I walked over to the wooden bench and sank down. Liam drifted beside me. Wound up, he talked continuously. I made do with a discreet nod or an "Um-hum," through my teeth.

Mary came back a half hour later. "The only records I could find were on Ulys Horntrop. He married a twenty five-year-old girl when he was fifty and produced three children." She shook her head. "Old geezer."

I agreed and held out my hand for the list. "Thanks a bunch."

"Just make sure I get a copy of the book," she called as I walked out.

I forced my grimace into a noncommittal smile.

"Well, we're down to four."

"Maybe," he acknowledged.

"We're missing something, aren't we?" I slid into the car as he opened the door, then slammed it.

"I think so, but I have no idea what." He glided in through the closed passenger window.

I started the car. "Do you want to swing by and see William?"

His face lit up. "Very much. Thank you."

"I don't want another run-in with the nosy neighbor or with the men in that dark alley. How about if I park the next block over? I'll walk slowly in front of the house to the end of the block and back. It won't give you much time, but at least you'll have a few minutes together."

"I'll make do."

I parked a block away. A black lab started barking from the fenced-in backyard as I stepped out of the car. Liam materialized in front of it.

Whimpering, it ran to the other side of the yard, its tail between its legs. Leaves rustled as a nearby squirrel leaned down from a leafy oak and chattered at the cowering dog. Liam came floating back. The lab stayed where it was.

"Neat trick. You're handy to have around."

"I'd like to see your human beaux do that." He whistled a jaunty tune.

"Beaux?" Enlightenment dawned. "Oh, you mean boyfriends? I don't have any boyfriends. I occasionally go out with Clayton. And I've been out a couple of times with Patrick."

"Clayton is an arse."

A giggle escaped. "You're right about that."

"Then why do you go out with him?" He glided beside me, his thumbs tucked into his waistband and his outlined defined.

"Habit, I guess."

"It's a habit you should break."

"Probably. Look we're here. See you soon."

"Soon." *Poof.* He disappeared.

"Now you see him, now you don't."

I continued at a sedate pace. The homes on the block were filled with flowers. I stopped and admired each one. I even complimented a woman who was on her knees digging industriously in the dirt around her roses.

I turned back at the end of the block, afraid if I went any farther I'd yank Liam out like a puppet on a string. I halted in front of William's house and watched a hummingbird stick his long beak into an azalea. When the tiny bird had drunk his fill, he flew away. I meandered to the car.

The door opened. "Well that's timing."

Liam didn't respond. His features drawn, he looked haggard.

"Liam?"

"William isn't doing well. He's not caught in the vortex of grief that Anna is, but he carries a heavy load of depression. He feels trapped, like there's no way out." Liam looked at me. His eyes grew intense and his color came back. "I told him you'd figure this out, that you would save him and Anna."

And lose you. Our glances held. The same thought reflected in his eyes that I knew was in my own. My heart ached. It was a physical pain, as if it had cracked a little on the inside.

What would I do without him? *I love you, Liam.* I bit my lip to keep from uttering the words. How had it happened? How had I allowed myself to fall in love with a ghost? I'd never been in love before, had no idea how deeply feelings ran, both hurtful and joyful. And Liam loved me too. I knew it, sensed it with every fiber of my being.

I cleared my throat. "Well then, we'd better work on getting you into the light."

He nodded. I slid into the seat. He closed the door and glided in through the closed window on the passenger side.

Neither of us talked as I merged into traffic. It must have been my preoccupation that caused me to miss the stop sign. Moments later, a siren whooped and lights flashed from a police car.

"Crap." I pulled over. "Dad's going to kill me."

Chapter 13

I reached for my license and got my registration out of the glove compartment before I rolled down my window.

"Ms. King."

Surprise jolted me. "Officer Atwell."

"You've got a different car." He grimaced as he looked at my bug.

What was it with guys and pink cars?

"The other was my mom's. Mine was in the shop." I gave the dashboard a loving pat.

"You look quite chic behind the wheel," he said gallantly.

He didn't look half bad himself. If I hadn't just discovered I was in love with a ghost, I would have been distracted by the long clean lines of him beneath his crisply pressed uniform.

"I didn't realize you were in town. I owe you a cup of coffee, remember?" He leaned his arms on the edge of the window.

"I'm afraid I lost your number." It seemed kinder to say than I'd forgotten all about him. If Liam hadn't dropped into my life, I would have called him.

He looked at his wristwatch. "I'll be off duty in a half hour. How about that coffee?"

"I wish I could, but I've got to be getting back."

"Can I call you?"

"Does getting a ticket hinge on my answer?"

"No. But you do need to pay more attention, although that overgrown bush does partially hide the stop sign." He gestured toward a large bright-leafed pachysandra.

"It does, doesn't it?" I brightened.

He leaned in closer. "Are you sure you can't stick around till I get off work?" He had a persuasive smile.

"I wish I could," I prevaricated. I couldn't deal with more testosterone right now, never mind that I had fallen in love with a ghost.

"That's twice now you've turned down a cup of coffee. Are you involved with someone?"

I took a deep breath. "Yes, I am."

"Caitlin," Liam whispered. His face held both triumph and sorrow.

"Can I call you? I know you just said you were involved, but a little healthy competition won't hurt whoever you're seeing. And if I can't win you away, I have no problem being friends with a beautiful woman."

My stomach muscles tightened. I didn't want to hurt anyone. "We live more than two hours apart."

"Can I call you?" he persisted.

I capitulated. "Of course, but don't expect anything from me. Life is complicated right now." I rattled off my cell number.

His eyes flashed and his grin widened. "Fair enough." He stood away from the car. "Drive carefully, Ms. King."

"I will, Officer Atwell." I eased forward. He raised his hand in acknowledgement. I raised mine, then concentrated on traffic.

"You collect beaux like a dog does fleas."

"That's a terrible analogy." Just thinking about it made me itch.

"You can't be involved with me." He took a deep breath, his eyes widened, and his voice remained carefully neutral. "Unless you were talking about Patrick."

"It's a little late for that don't you think? And no, I wasn't talking about Patrick." It would be so much easier if I were.

"Lass, what I have done to you?"

"Stolen my heart I'm afraid."

We had little to say on the ride home, both of us lost in our own thoughts. It was an unusual experience. Usually we chattered like magpies. The quiet of the car was laden, like a storm brewing, thick with tension that sucked one's breath right out.

I flipped on the radio and turned it to the Celtic station Liam liked. He threw me a quick smile before he went back to staring out the window. The trip that passed so quickly the other day seemed to last forever. Finally, we reached home, and I pulled in the garage beside the Vette.

"Don't worry, you'll have your life back soon." Liam floated to the door and opened it.

"That's what worries me," I whispered.

As we walked into the kitchen, Marcy dashed from the living room. "Where have you been?" Before I could respond, she rushed on. "Guess what I bought? Wait. I'll show you." She ran into the living room and came back with something behind her back.

"Ta da." She pulled it out with a flourish. "A Ouija board."

"Oh my God." I sank into the nearest chair.

"It'll be fun," she enthused. "Of course, we'll need to wait till it gets dark and light some candles."

"Of course."

Liam threw up his hands and shrugged.

The ringing of my cell distracted me. Thank goodness. The Ouija board made me nervous. I picked up my purse, which I'd tossed on the table, and dug it out. "Hello."

"Hi, Caitlin."

Delight rose in my throat and bubbled out my mouth. "Hi, Patrick." I might be in love with a ghost, but I liked a certain flesh and blood man...a lot.

"What are you doing?"

I walked into the living room and flopped down on the cushy couch. "I just got back from Ruby Falls."

"Research on your book?"

"Yeah."

"Have you eaten yet?"

"No." I glanced at my watch, surprised to see it was nearly five o'clock.

"Let me take you out then. Or you could invite me over and I'd bring a pizza."

"I can't tonight. I've got plans with my cousin." No way was I going to say it involved ghosts, candles, and Ouija boards.

"How about tomorrow night?"

"Sure."

"Do you want to go out, or shall I bring over a pizza and a couple of movies?"

"Pizza and movies sound great. About six?"

"I'll see you then."

I clicked off the phone just as the doorbell rang, then beat Liam to the door and opened it. A pimply face teen handed me a warm cardboard box. "Pizza delivery."

"Marcy, did you order a pizza?" I called.

"Sure did. Pay him, will you?"

I did as directed and took the box. The wonderful smells emanating from it made my knees weak. Pizza two nights in a row...couldn't beat it.

Caitlin walked in carrying a couple cans of Pepsi and napkins.

"Pizza was a great idea." I set the box on the coffee table and opened it. "Loaded. Yum." Like Pavlov's dog, saliva pooled in my mouth.

"You bet. We'll have a girls' night. After the pizza we'll play the Ouija board and maybe top off the evening with ice cream."

I took a bite of the steaming pie, briefly closing my eyes in ecstasy. "Okay," I mumbled around a mouthful. After all, it was just a game. What could possibly go wrong?

* * * *

With a sense of impending doom, I helped Marcy light the candles. I kept repeating to myself, *It's just a game. It's just a game.*

The little board that caused my heartburn—it couldn't possibly be from the four slices of pizza I ate—had black letters in the center and numbers beneath the letters.

Marcy turned out the lights.

"Okay, let's sit on the floor," she suggested.

I sat down and crossed my legs. She laid the board on our knees.

The board tilted as I shifted my legs. "Shouldn't we set the board on the floor?"

"The chances of making contact are better if it rests on our knees."

"Okay." The board jiggled as I moved closer.

"You have to be careful. Dropping the planchette can release evil spirits."

"We wouldn't want that." I'd tried for sarcasm, but since I meant it, I didn't quite pull it off.

She placed the planchette on the board. "Now the first thing we ask is, 'Ouija are you there?' Are you ready?"

I nodded.

"Ouija, are you there?" The candles flickered, but otherwise nothing happened.

Marcy cleared her throat and said louder. "Ouija, are you there?"

The planchette began to move. It went toward no, wavering before it did a sharp turn to yes.

"Did you do that?" Marcy asked excitedly.

"No. Did you?"

"No."

Liam hovered behind Marcy's shoulder. He winked at me and grinned.

Relief coursed through me. Just because there were ghosts, didn't mean Ouija boards could be used to contact spirits.

"It's the spirits," she whispered and looked around, her eyes sparkling. "What is my ghost's name?"

The planchette slid to the L, then I-A-M.

"Cat, you're doing that." Marcy glared at me.

I glared at Liam. With a flourish, he bowed and I swallowed a grin.

"Didn't you?" she huffed. Then, distracted, she asked, "What are you glaring at?"

"Nothing." Confirm or deny moving the planchette? Liam made the decision for me. The planchette slid to no.

"Cat?" Marcy tipped her head toward her shoulder and raised her eyebrows.

Mute, I shook my head. This was going to get dicey.

The planchette began to move. Since Marcy still glared at me, I didn't think she was moving it. The candle flames leaned to the right, then to the left in a macabre dance.

Liam shook his head, his eyes on the planchette. It began to move again. I relaxed my fingers as it hovered on the letter S. From S it moved to T.

I didn't like this. It slid to A. I put a bit more pressure on the planchette to try to control it as it landed on the Y. It stopped moving. Oh good.

"S-T-A-Y," Marcy spelled out. In spite of the pressure of my fingers, the planchette slid across the board. This time its stops were brief as if whoever guided the planchette was impatient for us to get his message.

"W-A-Y," Marcy spelled out loud.

A chill ran down my spine.

"Stay away." Marcy's eyes glowed with excitement, and she bounced up and down.

I grabbed the planchette as it started to slide. "Who are you?" I demanded.

"Why it's Liam, silly. Though I still can't figure out how you knew his name."

I ignored her and asked again, "Who are you?" My voice rose.

In a fighting stance, Liam turned in a slow circle. "I don't see him."

"Who are you?" My chest heaved and my breath came in short, sharp pants.

Marcy frowned at me, puzzled. "It's only a game."

I ignored her, my heart pounding and my palms sweating, and screamed. "Who are you?"

In fits and starts, the planchette started to move. E. I knew what was going to be spelled out. The planchette moved to Z. Intrigued, Marcy began to spell, "E-Z-R-A. Ezra?"

Goose bumps roughened my skin. The hair on the back of my neck rose. *Ezra Ames*. It had to be.

"Ezra, you have to let her go." I knew it was a mistake as soon as I said it, but there was no calling back the words.

A lamp flew across the room and missed my head by inches. Next, a lit candle whirled toward me. Liam grabbed it and put it out with his hand. "Leave her alone," he roared. In a nanosecond, he blew out the rest of the candles before Ezra could start a fire.

The television came on. Another lamp was hurled through the air.

"Shut the Ouija board," Liam yelled as he turned on the lights. They were immediately flicked off. The stereo blared.

I started to slam it shut.

"Say good-bye first," Marcy screamed.

"What?"

I ducked as a small ceramic horse flew off the shelf.

"You have to say good-bye. It's etiquette. If he doesn't respond, he might stay here."

"No, I'm pretty sure he won't," I yelled above the wind that whirled around us and slammed the board shut.

Everything quieted. The stereo clicked off. The wind died. The horse whirling through the air dropped to the floor.

Marcy looked at me and said with commendable calm. "Care to tell me what's going on?"

Chapter 14

"It's not like you haven't tried to tell her before," Liam grumbled as he toured the room.

"Maybe I should have tried harder. Is he gone?"

"Yes."

"Tried harder? What are you talking about?" Marcy asked confused. "And yes he appears to be gone. Would you please tell me what's going on?"

"Perhaps you'd better sit down."

"I am sitting down."

"So you are." I put the lamps back on the tables. Surprisingly, except for a dent in one of the shades, they weren't damaged. I collapsed back on the floor, my back against the couch. "Remember the other day when I told you the ghost's name was Liam?"

"Yeah, what a coincidence."

"No coincidence." I rubbed my forehead. I could feel a tension headache forming.

"What are you saying?"

"The ghost in the tube that wasn't damaged was Liam."

"So when you said you could see and hear the ghost, you were telling the truth, not studying lines for a play?"

"I tried to tell you."

"But not very hard."

"Not very hard," I admitted.

"So you are saying my ghost made this mess?" Marcy looked around in amazement.

"No! And he's not your ghost. He's mine," I snapped.

Liam studied me, a strange little smile on his features.

Heat flooded my face. I lifted my chin. He was my ghost. Mine. No matter what happened. No matter where he ended up, he was mine.

Marcy rubbed her chin with a well-manicured index finger and watched me as well. Finally she said, "This just isn't like you."

"What do you mean?"

"There's never been any rivalry between us about guys or objects. Even if I've had more than you, you've never cared."

"He's not an object," I said hotly. I could feel my eyes spark. I clenched my fists. "He's a living, breathing entity." Then, I amended, "Well maybe not the same as you or I live and breathe, but he's alive on his own plane. And the guys that dumped me to try to make headway with you were jerks. Good riddance to them."

She nodded in agreement.

"You can't have Liam. He's mine, Marcy."

"I am, lass, yours completely. I love you so much it makes my heart hurt." He had moved till he stood in front of me, his outline sharp and defined, emotion strong on his face.

My throat burned and my eyes stung. "And I'm yours," I whispered.

"We'll pretend that's the case for now. But you've got to remember it's temporary. I can't give you what you want and need." Misery crossed his strong-boned features.

"You're all I want." To my horror, I began to cry.

"Here now, lass. Please don't." Liam looked stricken and moved as close to me as he dared.

Marcy came over, put her arms around me, and hugged me before she handed me a tissue. I blew my nose, a loud honking sound, definitely not a feminine girlie-girl blow. Her features pasty white, she hurried to the phone and began to dial.

"Who are you calling," I blubbered.

"Your parents."

"No, no don't call my parents," I gurgled in alarm, trying to talk through the thickness in my throat.

The phone disappeared out of Marcy's hands and floated across the room. Marcy bit down on a shriek.

"It's okay. It's only Liam." I sniffled.

She took several deep breaths. "I get it. But seeing something float across the room is different than having something jerked out of your hands. Not to mention my fingers are tingling like I've had an electric shock." She shook her hand, her expression accusing.

Concern for my cousin made me forget about my woes. "I'm sorry. The tingling will disappear soon. Come into the kitchen and I'll fix you a cup of tea and tell you every single detail," I coaxed. "And this time I won't leave anything out."

"I'm thinking she needs something stronger," Liam observed.

"Since technically we're underage, nothing alcoholic is allowed in the house." I brushed at my wet cheeks.

"What?" Marcy stopped shrieking to look at me suspiciously.

"Liam thinks you need something stronger than tea." I guided her into the kitchen.

"He's got that right." She eyed the phone and shuddered.

I seated her at the table before I put the kettle on, then came back and sat down beside her. I squeezed her hand reassuringly. We sat that way for a moment, calming down as I tried to decide how I'd explain everything. Finally, I settled on starting at the beginning. "Remember the day the package arrived and you popped open the test tube?"

She nodded just as the teakettle began to sing. I put tea bags into the matching pink and brown polka dot mugs that said Marcy and Cat on one side and had pink sandals on the other.

I set the mugs on the table and slid into my seat. "I'll try to explain more fully. The moment you opened the test tube I smelled cinnamon and tart limes—Liam's signature fragrance—and felt a surge of electricity."

"But you never said anything."

"I didn't know if it was anything more than my imagination. That night when I thought there was an intruder…"

"Liam?"

"Yes, Liam."

"I still don't understand, why didn't you tell me? We tell each other everything." She looked hurt.

"I should have. I'm sorry. I just couldn't bring myself to share him, even with you."

"I see." A little smile played on her face, her gaze perceptive. She looked around. "Is he here now?"

Liam had floated into one of the other chairs. His elbows on the table, he swiveled his head back and forth between the two of us, rapt attention on his features.

I pointed toward him.

"So all the times you were practicing your lines, you were talking to Liam."

"Yeah."

Her eyes narrowed. "And the time I got an electric shock from the pool chair?"

"You sat on him."

"My apologies. It wasn't very gentlemanly of me." Liam looked chagrined.

"He apologizes."

"What about the other test tube?" She pulled a delicate white ceramic sugar bowl toward her and put enough sugar in her tea to make a Northerner wince.

"That gets a bit tricky," I admitted as she passed me the sugar bowl. I added several heaping teaspoons to my tea and sipped. "The broken test tube held his twin, who escaped en route when the test tube broke."

"Really?" she breathed.

"Yeah."

"Was it his sister who threw things around tonight?" She set down the mug and wrapped her hands around it as she kept glancing at the empty chair where Liam sat.

"No. But there's a connection. Both Liam and his sister were killed on her wedding day. She loved Wil—"

"Don't say it," Liam shouted, jumping out of the chair and waving his arms.

"Right."

"She loved her fiancé so much she refused to move into the light and leave him, so she's caught in a vortex looking for him."

"Oh, the poor thing." Marcy's eyes filled with tears. "And Liam?" She sniffed and wiped her eyes.

I tipped my cup. The caramel-colored liquid swirled in circles round and around. Finally, I said, "He wouldn't leave her behind."

Her eyes widened. "That's truly heroic."

"One of the most heroic things I've ever heard," I agreed.

"Cut that stuff out, you're embarrassing me," my ghost grumbled. His face glowed bright red.

"We're embarrassing him."

"Really?" She looked at the empty chair, then back at me. "So you can see and hear him?"

"Yeah."

"I'd love to see what he looks like." Marcy rested her chin in her hand, her voice wistful.

"Be right back." I hopped up. My heart expanded and warmth flooded me. Finally, something about Liam I could share with Marcy. "Where did I leave my purse…. Oh yeah." It was at the other end of the table near Liam. Duh.

"Would you toss me my purse?" I was showing off, but I couldn't help it.

He grinned at me and slid it across the table. Maybe he was showing off a bit too.

Marcy's jaw dropped. "I'm not sure I can get used to this."

"You will. Trust me." I dug out my phone, punched up the picture of Liam with his horse, and handed it to her. I couldn't wait to see her reaction.

"This is Liam?" She blinked, then stared.

"Yes."

"What a hottie." She glanced at the empty chair. "Liam, you're worth every penny of the three thousand I paid for you."

I burst into laughter and couldn't stop. My stomach hurt I laughed so much. Leave it to Marcy. Liam's chair, which he'd balanced on two legs, came down with a thump. After one startled moment, Liam laughed too.

While I regained control, Marcy reached for her tea and sipped it thoughtfully. "I need chocolate." Her chair scraped against the floor as she pushed it back. "What happened to Liam's twin's fiancé? By the way, what's her name?" She rummaged in the pantry, pulled out a couple of Swiss chocolate bars, and tossed me one.

"Her name's Anna. And her fiancé is like Liam. He won't cross over without her, either." I spoke thickly around a mouthful of chocolate.

"So what's keeping them apart?"

"Ezra Ames," Liam and I said in unison.

"I never saw that one coming." Liam leaned back in his chair and stared at the ceiling.

"I did," I said smugly. "In the church picture, he was looking at Anna the way she was looking at Wil—"

"Don't say it," Liam interrupted.

"Can't link their names or Ezra goes on a tear," I told Marcy, who looked understandably lost. I'd finished the chocolate bar in record time so I yanked a daisy out of the fresh flowers that sat on the kitchen table and began to pluck at the petals.

Marcy got up, trotted to the cabinet, and threw me another candy bar. "Don't decapitate the poor flowers."

"Sorry." I ripped open the wrapper and crammed a large piece in my mouth.

"This is unbelievable. You should write a book."

I choked, then swallowed. "Thinking seriously about it."

"What happens now?" Marcy'd grabbed another chocolate bar for herself as well. She sat down and began to unwrap it.

"Now that we know who it is, we've got to convince him to let Anna and her fiancé reunite. I'm just not sure how to approach it without him destroying the house." A chocolate smear was on my blouse. I scraped at it with my nails, but it didn't come off.

Marcy chewed on her chocolate and stared into space. "The Ouija Board almost worked. But we need something stronger when trying to contact the spirits. We'll hold a séance."

Chapter 15

I spent the night and the next day trying to think of a good excuse not to have it. I didn't want to lose Liam. It was small and selfish of me, but there it was. Unfortunately, it didn't matter. We had to do this. If I truly loved Liam, I'd let him go. And Anna and her beloved William had been apart too long.

The doorbell rang as we prepped for the séance.

"Who could that be?" Marcy asked.

"I forgot to tell you Patrick picked up a couple movies and a pizza. Why don't you stick around and join us?"

"Three's a crowd." She waved her hand airily.

"Then stay and we'll have a foursome," I said dryly and headed for the door.

Marcy giggled. "Okay with you?" she asked the air.

"The more the merrier," Liam replied, floating with me to the door.

"He'd love for you to stay," I responded. I'd gone from talking to a ghost to acting as interpreter for his and Marcy's conversations. They were getting along like a house on fire.

I opened the door. Patrick balanced a large pizza box in one hand and held movies in the other. He wore jeans with a hole in the knee and a faded gray T-shirt.

"Come in."

As he entered, the smell of sauce and herbs mingled with soap and clean cotton.

"Hi there." He looked me over and smiled appreciatively. "You look great. But then you always do."

"Thanks." I wore a pair of jean shorts, a plain white silk tee with a scooped neck, and black thong sandals with white bows.

"He's right, lass, you look…"

"A fair treat," I mouthed under my breath.

"I was going to say fair beautiful, but fair treat works."

We smiled at each other.

Patrick gave me a puzzled look. I came back to reality with a thump and headed for the living room. Marcy came out of the kitchen carrying a tray loaded with cans of soda, mauve and white striped paper plates, and matching napkins and cups filled with ice, the paper the same color as Marcy's mauve tee.

"Nice accessorizing."

"Thank you."

"Marcy's joining us," I told Patrick as I placed the warm cardboard box on the coffee table.

"Perfect, I'll get to spend the evening with two lovely ladies." He smiled at Marcy, a friendly smile that held no intimacy, before he turned and looked at me. His eyes lit up and guilt seized me. Patrick was a good man. I didn't want to hurt him. And right now the only man I wanted in my life was my ghost. I had a sinking feeling that wasn't going to change, even when he left me.

"Hey, Cat, you okay?" Patrick tapped my elbow.

"Oh, yeah." I shifted toward him.

"Sometimes you just go away. You're with me one minute and the next, it's like you're someplace else."

That brought me back. "Just spacing. Underneath the black is pure blonde." I pointed at my head and laughed.

"No. You're a very intelligent woman. I'm not sure why you'd want to hide it." He didn't smile, just studied me. Frown lines wrinkled his brow.

Marce glanced at Patrick, then me. "Let's eat this while it's hot." Steam rose in a warm, sensuous tide of mouthwatering scents.

Thank you, Marcy.

"Patrick, plug in a movie," she ordered.

"I brought a chick flick and a comedy. Which do you want to see first?"

"You brought a chick flick?" Marce and I asked in unison.

"Trying to score points." He grinned.

"Chick flick?" Liam asked, puzzled.

I cleared my throat. "Picking up a movie aimed for a female audience definitely gets you points."

"Oh, I see." Liam nodded. "Smart move."

I did a mental eye roll. Guys.

As the previews rolled, we settled on the couch. Liam stretched out about a foot above the back of it, his legs crossed, his chin resting in his palm. He'd tossed his jacket over the chair.

The background music of the movie nearly drowned out the doorbell.

Marcy and I looked at each other. I shook my head and hunched my shoulders.

"I'll get it." Pizza in hand, she pushed up from the couch.

Liam floated after her. In a few moments, he drifted back, a scowl on his face. "You really need to get rid of that one," he said, clueing me in to our visitor's identity.

"Look who dropped by," Marcy said in a cheery voice, a bright smile plastered on her face.

"Hello, Clayton," I said with a notable lack of enthusiasm.

Clayton's gaze swept our cozy little tableau. "Caitlin," he said, his manner stiff.

I stood up, Patrick rose, and I made the introductions. The men clasped hands and studied each other. Clayton grimaced and flexed his fingers as he pulled his hand back. "Caitlin, can I talk to you a moment?"

"Sure." I headed for the kitchen.

"Is that the boyfriend?" Patrick asked. I didn't hear Marcy's reply.

When we got to the kitchen, Clayton snapped out, "Who is that?"

I hadn't noticed that Liam had come with us. I shouldn't have been surprised. He circled Clayton. "I don't like his tone."

"I don't either." My back straightened and my body stiffened.

"Excuse me?" Clayton arched an eyebrow.

"I said it's none of your business."

"No, you didn't. You said 'I don't either.'" Confusion had replaced stiffness.

"What do you want?"

"I hadn't seen you in a while so I thought I'd stop by and say hello. Are you dating that guy?" His jaw jutted, he leaned forward.

"And if I am? We're not an item, Clayton, remember? You see other people. Well I'm seeing someone else, too."

"You're trying to make me jealous, aren't you? Well it worked, darling." He reached for me.

I stepped back.

"What a pompous ass." Liam's features were sharp and defined. Electricity crackled off him. He rolled his fingers against his palms, a look of anticipation on his handsome features.

Uh-oh.

"No, I'm not trying to make you jealous."

The pompous ass dropped his arms, but his expression remained confident. My ghost was bouncing up and down on his toes, the light of battle in his eyes. Unease tightened my tummy.

"Is it because I haven't been around in a while?"

I'd never noticed quite how conceited Clayton was. I'd never been interested enough to find out. "No. It's because I like Patrick. He's nice and he's fun."

"Come on, he's not one of us."

"Not...one of us?"

He continued as if I hadn't spoken. "Well, slum all you want now, but once we're engaged that will have to come to a halt."

"Engaged," I shrieked. "Are you delusional?"

"Oh, come now. You must know it's what your uncle wants."

"If you think marrying me will cement your banking career with my uncle, you are sadly mistaken. And if it's your job you're so concerned about, why didn't you go after Marcy?"

His eyes shifted.

"You did, didn't you? When?"

"It was a long time ago."

Great. Another of Marcy's castoffs. Why hadn't she told me?

"You need to leave."

"I understand you're upset."

"Now." I gritted my teeth and jammed my fists in my pockets, forcing myself to stay calm. Momma would be appalled if I hit him.

"You heard the lady." Liam took Clayton by the collar and hauled him through the house toward the front room.

I hopped in front of them, raced for the door, and threw it open.

Patrick and Marcy came to their feet as Clayton went stumbling by, his arms flailing, yelling, "What's going on? What's going on?"

Eyes wide, Marcy put her hand over her mouth.

Patrick started forward, but he wasn't quick enough.

"Goodnight, Clayton." I shut the door on him and leaned against it.

"I'd had all of that sanctimonious horse's arse I could take." Liam glared at me, his arms crossed.

I bit my lips together. My shoulders shook as I began to giggle. The giggles escalated until tears ran down my cheeks. Then, I stopped laughing but the tears continued. Thick and hot, they dripped down my face.

"Caitlin." That was all Patrick said. He took me in his arms and held me. Liam watched, his expression unbearably sad.

"What did the bastard say to upset you?" Patrick murmured.

I shook my head, grateful he refrained from asking why the bastard left flapping his arms.

"Perhaps, I should go teach preppie some manners."

"Take a number." I began to giggle again. Patrick's arms tightened. Once I got myself under control, I stepped back and sniffed loudly. Marcy handed me a tissue.

"Are you okay?" Patrick asked.

"Yes." I sniffled.

"I should go home."

"I'm sorry, Patrick. But it might be best. I'd be pretty lousy company."

"No problem. I'll give you a call." He leaned forward and gave me a chaste kiss on the forehead.

My nerves tightened as apprehension filled me. Liam's gaze shifted away from mine. This time there had been no electrical surge when Patrick touched me.

"Patrick?" Marcy stepped forward.

"Yes?" Patrick turned to her, but he continued to glance back at me, concerned.

"Could you come back tomorrow night about eight o'clock?" Marcy opened the door.

"Sure. What's up?"

"We're going to have a séance."

My insides iced and my legs tingled. My breath stuck in my throat.

Liam stared at Marcy.

"Well?" She smiled at Patrick, her head tipped, her hands on her hips, as if she hadn't just dropped a bomb on us.

"Never a dull moment at this house," he observed. "See you tomorrow night."

As soon he left, I turned on my cousin. "This isn't a good idea."

"It's time for Liam, Anna, and her friend to move on, sweetie."

The expression in Liam's eyes was poignant. I forced myself to pay attention to Marcy.

"I found someone reputable. I spent most of the day checking her out. Now tell me what happened in the kitchen."

"When Clayton said I'd need to stop slumming after we were engaged, Liam grabbed him by the collar and marched him out the door." I started to giggle again, then sobered. "Why didn't you tell me Clayton came on to you?"

"Clayton asked me out a long time ago." She made a dismissive gesture with her hand. "When you first started seeing each other, you were at loose ends. I didn't see where it would hurt anything. If I'd realized what a complete ass he is, I would have warned you off. And thank goodness I didn't."

"Why not?"

"I wouldn't have gotten to see that fascinating exit." She chuckled.

A grin tugged at the corner of my mouth. "There is that. Marcy…"

"Hmm?" She'd sat back down and reached for the remote. "I'm going to rewind the movie. Though, I'm sure it won't be nearly as engrossing as our evening has been thus far. By the way, Liam, well done."

He grinned.

"Marcy," I said again.

"What?"

"If you're sure you want to do this, there're a couple of people I'd like to invite." I proceeded to tell her about the two friends I'd made in Ruby Falls.

"That's a great idea. Not counting Liam, that'll make six of us."

"Tell me again what your cousin is planning to do." Liam was once again stretched out a foot above the couch, ankles crossed, his hand propping up his head.

"She's contacted a medium to try to make contact and…" The words stuck in my throat. I swallowed and continued, "Send you into the light." I bit my lips together, determined not to do anything stupid, like cry. This was what I wanted for Liam. This was what would be best for him. But not for me.

"Well if a spiritualist couldn't help Lincoln's wife, I don't see them doing much for a Johnny Reb," he grumbled.

"I'd forgotten about that."

"What are you talking about?" Marcy asked curiously.

"Mary Todd Lincoln used a spiritualist on the death of her son. Lincoln came to some of the séances."

"Cool."

"It didn't help her any." Liam floated from his place above the couch nearer to the ceiling.

"It didn't help her any," I parroted.

"But we think we know who is standing between Anna and—"

"Don't say it," Liam and I cautioned at the same time.

"And her fiancé," Marcy finished up. "What's the worst that can happen?"

"Ezra destroys us," I said and reached for a piece of cold pizza.

Chapter 16

The next evening found me trying to rub away a headache forming between my eyes. After eighteen years of interacting with Marcy, I knew the futility of arguing once she'd made up her mind. She wanted this séance to be an event. I just wanted it over.

It was nearly seven-thirty. I'd called Aileen and Ethel. They'd accepted with alacrity and promised to be here before eight.

Dark blue candles sat in the center of the table. The scent of incense wafted from a burner on the mantle. A mahogany espresso end table held a bowl of crystals. Refreshments covered the kitchen bar. I had balked at the hors d'oeuvres, but Marcy assured me refreshments were offered at all the best séances. I bowed to her wisdom.

Sasha Blaine, or Madam Sasha as Marcy called her, would be arriving any minute. I walked around the dining room where Marcy had decided to hold the séance.

The fan overhead circulated the air and caused the candle flames to sway. It also brought the scent of cinnamon and limes. Liam strode back and forth around the room a foot off the ground, muttering.

"What if it works?" he demanded, stopping in front of me.

"Do you think it will?" My heart tightened. Coldness permeated me to the bone, and I rubbed my arms trying to warm myself.

"Yes. No. I don't know." He threw up his hands. "It didn't work for Mary Todd Lincoln."

If I had a dollar for every time I'd heard that in the past twenty-four hours. "She was a Yankee."

He stopped his pacing and grinned. "So she was."

"Are we ready?" Marcy strolled into the dining room. She wore a black scarf, pulled over her forehead and tied behind her head. A white, low-cut peasant blouse showed off her honey-colored skin, and a black and red silk skirt swished when she walked. Her feet were bare. All she needed was a tambourine.

"All she needs is a tambourine," Liam said.

I swallowed a laugh. "Nice look, Marcy. Of course, you can make an elongated paper bag look good."

"You like it?" She swirled around and bells jingled. For the first time, I noticed them sewn to the bottom of her hem.

"It should get the spirits moving, at least the guys." A giggle tickled my throat.

"Why thank you. What do you think, Liam?" She spoke to the air in the opposite direction of where he stood.

"Very fetching."

"Very fetching," I repeated.

"Thank you."

She glanced at me from head to toe. "Very twenty-first century, Caitlin."

I wore black jeans, a black silk blouse, and a long rainbow moonstone necklace. I fingered the stones, hoping their positive energy would see me through the night. Before I could respond, the doorbell rang.

"That's Madam Sasha." The bells on Marcy's skirt tinkled as she turned to hurry out. When she got to the arch, she shifted in my direction, her manner somber. "Good luck tonight, Liam."

"Thanks. And thank you for what you're doing. If it works, I'll be eternally in your debt."

"He thanks you, and if it works, he'll be eternally yours," I loosely translated.

"That's not quite what I said," he protested.

"Promises, promises." Marcy gave an airy wave and disappeared through the doorway.

Liam stood so close the energy around him warmed my skin and gave me a pleasurable tinge.

"Lass." He reached out a hand.

I held my breath. I wanted him to touch me so badly it hurt. He dropped his hand and sighed. "For Anna's sake, I want this to work. For mine... I don't know if I can bear it. But you listen to me. If it does work, I want you to get on with your life."

"Stay," I whispered. I hadn't meant to say it, would have bitten off my tongue if I could have prevented it. But the word was out before I could call it back.

His tortured countenance mirrored the agony building inside me. "I can't do anything for ye. If I move on tonight, you need to forget me and find someone else."

"I don't want anyone else." Tears stung my eyes.

"Lass, I couldn't make love with you. I couldn't give you children."

"I could adopt." I cringed as the words slipped out, appalled that I was making this evening harder for him. But I couldn't seem to stop.

He tried for a lighter note. "And how would I discipline the little beggars? An electric shock to their hindquarters?"

"I don't believe in corporal punishment."

"Ye are missing the point." He clutched his head.

"Liam, you're my world. I don't care if I never have sex or children as long as I have you." My breath came in deep sharp pants. I needed a paper bag.

"Calm down, lass. What's the chance of this even working?" His tone was soothing, his features relaxed. But he didn't fool me. His form was sharp and clear, more defined than usual. The cords in his neck stood out and a tic was visible in his jaw.

"Right, you're right." I stopped my mental hand wringing. If he could give the appearance of calm, I could at least try to do the same.

"You didn't mention that someone in the house had already made contact." The voice that came from behind me was low and rich, filled with magnetic energy.

Heat crept up my cheeks. I batted it down. After all, she was supposed to be a medium.

She came forward and extended her hand. "I'm Sasha Blaine."

She wasn't at all what I'd expected. Sasha Blaine wore a tailored white suit with a gold silk shell underneath the jacket and a string of pearls. Low black pumps, simple enough to be very expensive, encased her feet. She could have been anywhere between thirty and sixty. Her chestnut-colored hair was cut in a sleek bob and liberally streaked with gray, her face devoid of makeup.

"Caitlin King." I held out my hand.

Hers closed over mine. Electricity sang up my arms. Oh boy, this was the real deal.

"What is it you are hoping to accomplish tonight?" Her voice, while charged with energy, soothed. I held onto her hand like a lifeline. Strength of purpose flowed through me. I took a deep steadying breath. "Reunite two lovers and send three souls into the light. Maybe four," I amended, thinking of Ezra.

"Then we'll see what we can do."

The doorbell rang again. Marcy smiled encouragingly at me and slipped out to answer the door. Ethel and Aileen walked in chattering, their voices filled with excitement.

"Here, I thought these might help." Ethel thrust two pictures at me. One was of Liam. The other was of the church picnic, which had William, Anna, and Ezra in it.

"May I see?" Sasha held out her hand.

She took the picture of Liam, held it between her hands, and closed her eyes. When she opened them, she looked at me. "He's with us and he loves you, very much."

My throat constricted and my eyes stung.

"Oh my," Aileen breathed.

She hadn't seen that one coming.

Sasha set the picture on the table and took the other. Aileen and Ethel clasped hands. Marcy leaned forward, engrossed. I held my breath.

"I feel—" Sasha began. The doorbell rang again.

My breath went out in a whoosh. "That will be Patrick."

I hurried to the door.

He stood on the stoop, in clean jeans and a forest green Henley, holding daisies. "I don't know if they're appropriate for a séance, but they're for you. I should have brought some for Marcy, but I didn't think of it."

"Thank you. They're beautiful. Please come in." I stepped back and he walked in. He seemed so comfortable and solid after dealing with spirits and lacerated emotions. I buried my nose in the flowers. They smelled of sunlight instead of dark and ethereal beings.

Everyone had moved into the kitchen where they all talked at once. Marcy, the perfect Southern hostess, was pouring coffee and passing out cookies. "Hi, Patrick." She gave him a bright smile.

"Hi, Marcy." He smiled back and ambled toward her. She handed him a cup of coffee and a plate heaped with cookies.

"Thanks." He set the plate down and popped a cookie in his mouth.

"The flowers are beautiful. How did you know Caitlin loves daisies?"

I liked all flowers, but Marcy was nothing if not diplomatic.

He swallowed the cookie and wiped crumbs off his upper lip before he responded. "They remind me of her, pert and pretty, like sunshine."

"Nicely said," Marcy complimented. "Let me introduce you to everyone while Caitlin sees to her flowers." Patrick grabbed his plate of cookies.

I got a crystal vase out of the cabinet while Marcy took Patrick's arm and made the introductions.

The group prattled on, except for Sasha, who remained unruffled, answering questions in her calm way. "This is a good group. Everyone here has an open mind. Shall we begin?"

As the others trooped into the dining room, I mouthed to Liam, "I love you."

"I know, lass." His stormy eyes grew dark and intense, like waves crashing against the shore.

Patrick stood in the entryway. "Are you ready, Caitlin?"

If he'd seen anything, he didn't let on. And at this point, if he had, did it really matter?

We walked into the dining room together. As Patrick and I strode through the entryway, Liam passed through the wall. The others were already seated. There was one seat open at the end of the table and one beside Sasha.

"Caitlin, please sit beside me." Sasha pointed to the empty spot. Patrick walked to the end of the table and pulled out a chair.

Liam moved to stand behind me. The sharp scent of limes and cinnamon surrounded me, more tangy than usual. Nerves skittered up my spine. What if Sasha really found a way to send him back? I needed him to reassure me everything would be okay.

As if he knew, he moved closer. Electricity ricocheted around me. It enveloped and energized me. For a moment, sadness darkened his eyes before he winked and gave me a thumbs up. I forced my clenched jaws loose and smiled.

Her countenance calm, Sasha watched me, her dark brown eyes filled with knowledge. Again I thought, she was the real deal.

Ethel and Aileen talked in low animated voices. Marcy leaned forward to chat with Patrick. Their chatter faded into the background as Sasha's magnetic gaze drew me in. "You've already made contact." It was a statement, not a question.

I cleared my throat. "It's not the spirit we're trying to contact."

She reached over and picked up the photographs that Ethel had brought and laid them on the table. Then she placed her hand on the pictures, took a deep breath, and closed her eyes.

Everyone stopped talking. The room grew quiet. All was silent except for a light swish of material and a low tinkle from a single bell as Marcy shifted in her seat. We held our collective breaths. Only Ethel's features registered dismay, and I had no doubt that had to do with someone touching the pictures.

Several moments passed. Finally, Sasha spoke, her eyes still closed. "Your spirit has a strong presence. He's a good man. He wants his sister to move into the light, but he is reluctant to leave you."

My gaze shifted and collided with Liam's. He now stood on the table near the flame of the candles. His gaze held mine, his face somber.

"Oh, how romantic," Ethel whispered.

"Everyone please be quiet," Sasha murmured. She placed both hands on the group photograph. She ran her index finger over everyone in the picture. "Anna, your visitant spirit's sister, mourns for her fiancé, William. William mourns for Anna."

The lights flickered and thunder rumbled. Uh-oh. My gaze flew to Liam.

"At least she didn't mention uniting them." Liam jumped to the floor and moved to the table's edge next to me. He leaned his hips against it and braced a hand on the table.

I inhaled his sensual scent. My skin tingled with the light rush of electricity his nearness always brought.

"The man who stands between them is near. He's a boy really. Afraid to join us, afraid we'll make fun of him, that he won't be welcome.

"Anna was the only one that ever cared about him. If she goes to William, she won't want him anymore. The day she was going to marry, she was leaving him, going to William. If he lets her go now, he'll be alone throughout eternity, surrounded by darkness with no one."

The words tore at me. Poor, unloved boy. "What happened to him?" I whispered.

"He died of scarlet fever a year after Anna passed."

On impulse, I put my hand over Sasha's, then clutched it to keep from drawing back. Nerves skittered and jumped under her skin. Power surged through her.

"Of course she'll still care about you, Ezra. You can go with her, with Anna, William and"—my voice cracked—"Liam. You'll live with the angels, Ezra. They'll take care of you."

The atmosphere grew heavy. Tension built like a low rolling raincloud.

"He wants to believe you, but he's afraid it's a trick." The thick air grew chill. Goose bumps popped up on my skin. I'd never be warm again.

"Tell him, Liam," I whispered.

"Ezra, my sister doesn't have a mean bone in her body. Of course she'd let you stay with her. It's time we all moved into the light."

My hand dropped away. Sasha stretched out her arms and threw back her head. "Anna and William, make your presence known. Come to those in this circle so we can guide you to the next cycle of your journey. We will send you into the light."

The faces around me lost all color. Marcy's eyes grew huge.

I grabbed the table. My fingers tightened around the edge of the smooth wood. The angles of Liam's face, especially his cheekbones, were sharp and prominent, blood red in color. He wore a look of tense expectancy. My breath went out in a whoosh as I watched it change from one of edgy anticipation to a joy and beauty that took my breath away.

I couldn't see anything. I leaned toward Liam. "Is it Anna?"

"Yes, with William. They're walking hand in hand. She's motioning for Ezra to come with them, and she's holding a hand out to me."

A golden glow surrounded him. He made no move to go to his sister. I knew what held him back…me.

I swallowed and tried to speak. Nothing came out. I tried again. This time I forced out, "Go. Don't make them wait again."

He looked at me, the light surrounding him blinding. "I love you. I'll always carry you in my heart, Caitlin King, and I can see I'll always be in yours. But promise me you'll live life to the fullest and be happy. Promise me."

Or you'd never leave me, would you? I bit my lips hard and nodded.

He stepped through the air and turned. For one brief moment, they were all together and visible. Anna and William, their arms around each other, their faces glowing with love and happiness, Ezra standing behind Anna, smiling, his face looking at something I couldn't see. I hoped it was the angels. And my Liam, his hand in his sister's. "Promise me." His gaze held mine.

"I promise," I whispered, my fingers crossed behind my back.

Electricity snapped through the room and they were gone.

The room spun madly. My heart ached. My throat closed. For one crazy moment, I wondered if I was having a heart attack. And then, for the first and only time in my life, I fainted.

Chapter 17

Strong arms circled me. Something thumped erratically against my ear. I hovered just below consciousness. I should have pushed myself to awareness, but the knowledge of something too painful to be born held me back.

"Take her into the bedroom." I recognized Marcy's voice.

"Is she all right?" Patrick sounded anxious and strained. Voices murmured in the background, a low hum like a swarm of bees.

"She's had a shock. But she's strong, she'll recover." The voice was familiar, but I wasn't certain who it belonged to, nor did I want to know. If I remembered who, I'd remember other things as well.

Patrick's arms tightened. He scooped me up against his chest and strode out of the room. Moments later, my head hit the pillow. The cool cotton beneath my cheek made me shiver. The cold permeated my bones. Would I ever feel warm again?

"I'll call her tomorrow." Silence followed for a heartbeat. "I don't know how to compete with a ghost."

"Just give her time, Patrick." Marcy's voice came from a long way off.

Ghost? Liam! Pain hit me from all sides. I couldn't breathe, then decided not to try as I hurled down into blackness.

* * * *

I don't know how long I slept, just that whenever I came close to consciousness, my mind shut down.

"Come on, honey, you've slept on and off for three days. Your mom's called several times. Patrick wanted to call an ambulance, but I wouldn't let him. I knew you'd snap out of it. By the way, it's Sunday, brunch day." Damp heat mixed with the scent of strong aromatic coffee tickled my nose.

My hands shaking, I pushed up and reached for the coffee Marcy held under my nose. I took a sip, then set the cup on the bedside table and stretched. "Hi," I croaked.

"Hi." A frown of concern wrinkled her brow and marred her normally cheerful countenance.

I looked around for Liam. *Liam.* There was no more Liam. My breath caught in my throat and I began to hyperventilate. I couldn't breathe. Harsh rasping sounds came from my throat.

"Put your head down." Not waiting to see if I obeyed, Marcy shoved my head between my knees. My closed lungs opened. I pushed Marcy's hands away and sat up, my breath uneven and sharp.

With a sympathetic smile, she reached over and touched my hand. "I know this is difficult for you. I'm going to miss our ghost too."

I knew she meant well, was trying to comfort me. But I'd passed the rational stage when Liam left me.

"He was never your ghost. Don't you understand?" My voice rose. "He came to me." I fisted my hand against my heart. "Me." My voice cracked and to my horror, I broke into harsh, noisy sobs.

"It's okay, honey. It's okay." Marcy leaned over, scooped me up, and rocked me back and forth.

I cried till Marcy's shirt was soaked and there was no liquid left, till my tear ducts clogged and my eyelids swelled.

I pulled back and wiped my face with the edge of my shirt. She handed me a tissue and I blew noisily, before pushing to my feet. "Thanks. I didn't mean to be such a bitch. But you know what you said about it being okay?"

She nodded, head slightly turned, her eyes narrowed.

"I'm not sure it will ever be okay, at least not for the next fifty or sixty years." I twisted the soggy tissue into a ball.

"I'm so sorry. I don't know what to say or do to make things better for you. Do you want me to tell the folks you're sick and skip the brunch?"

For half a second I gave it serious thought before I shook my head. "Mom and Aunt Janet would both be over here fussing like two mother hens. I better get it over with."

"I'll let you get ready." She touched my arm before she walked away. At the doorway, she paused and turned. "I'm truly sorry. I know you loved him."

Unable to speak, I nodded and headed for the bathroom. One look in the mirror told me my face looked every bit as bad as I'd anticipated.

The splotchy-faced stranger who looked back at me had dull, red-rimmed eyes. *Suck it up, Caitlin, the world hasn't ended.* But it had. I wanted to scream. I wanted to cry. My head pounded with a dull constant throb.

I turned the water in the shower on as hot as it would go and climbed in. The scalding drops beat against my body and I welcomed the heat, hoping it would drive out the cold. It didn't.

I raised my head and sniffed the air, but there was no lime and cinnamon, only the cherry vanilla scent of the shower gel. He was gone.

My tear ducts weren't clogged after all. Hot droplets spurted from my eyes and mingled with the sharp spray of water that ran in rivulets down my face.

When there was no more hot water, I dragged myself from the marble-tiled stall. Dense condensation filled the room. I looked around helplessly. All I wanted to do was climb back in bed. Instead, I wiped the mist from the mirror and leaned into it. "You can do this."

Splashing cold water on my face, I did the best I could to hide the ravages of weeping. It took me a long time to get ready. My clothes weighed me down. Everything was an effort, even running a brush through my hair. Finally ready, I stepped out of the bedroom to meet Marcy. We'd both worn black.

* * * *

Conversation at the dinner table ebbed and flowed around me. Marcy nudged me at appropriate moments and I'd nod. The peas on my plate looked like tiny green marbles I pushed around with my fork. My eyes pooled when I looked at the gravy covering my mashed potatoes and remembered Liam and the gravy boat.

"What the hell is wrong with you, Caitlin?" Dad asked. "This is the third time your mom has asked you the same question."

"Wh-what?" I stammered.

"What's wrong with you? Why is your face all red and blotchy? Why aren't you talking?" The questions came rat-a-tat-tat, bulleted at me like the journalist he was.

"Noth—" To my intense embarrassment the tears so near the surface swelled and spilled over.

"Caitlin?" He tossed down his napkin and started to rise from his chair.

I jumped out of mine. As I headed for the door, Dad asked, "She's not pregnant, is she?" Every father's secret nightmare.

"From a ghost?" Marcy responded.

Oh my God. I fled the house.

My sides heaving, I made my way to the back of our little cottage and slid into a lounge chair where I stared at the glistening water. This place always brought me comfort. I leaned back, closed my eyes, and let the sun warm me. Slowly, the shudders wracking my body subsided. I pretended Liam was beside me in the other chair.

"Caitlin." My father's voice was gentle.

"Hmm?" I didn't open my eyes, holding tight to my hard won control. The other chair creaked. I winced. Liam should have been lounging in that chair.

My father took my hand, gave a light squeeze, and let go. "Can you tell me about it?"

"No," I whispered.

"I'm a good listener."

He'd never believe me. "I know you are."

"Was your ghost in the kitchen the day Vel nearly dropped the gravy boat?"

My eyes flew open.

His hands clasped, Dad leaned toward me. His face held concern but none of the skepticism I'd expected.

"If I said I'd seen and conversed with a ghost, you'd believe me?" I shaded my eyes from the sun's glare.

"Honey, if you told me the sun rose in the west, I'd believe you." He said it simply, his features sincere.

"Oh, Dad." I stumbled out of the chaise and into his arms. He pulled me down beside him.

"Hush, baby, it's okay."

"Why do people keep saying that? It's not okay. It's not going to be okay."

He sighed and patted my shoulder.

I took a shuddering breath and straightened. He handed me a pristine white handkerchief. I honked into it.

"There's my girl. Now tell me what happened."

I told him all of it, ending with, "I fell in love with a ghost. How crazy is that?" I picked at the edges of the soggy handkerchief.

"Do you realize how lucky you are?"

"Lucky?"

"On so many levels. You got to see into a dimension that people have never been sure existed. And you saved two tormented souls. You united them, let them finally be together."

The knot in my belly loosened. I leaned over and hugged him. "I love you, Dad." His hard, warm arms circled me. His heart beat steady against my ear. For just a moment, I was his little girl again, safe in those arms where nothing could harm me. "You would have liked him."

"I'm sure I would."

"Would you like to see his picture?"

Dad threw me a startled look. "How would I do that?"

I pulled my phone out of my little black clutch purse. "There was a picture of him at the Preservation Library in Ruby Falls." My insides warmed at the picture of my ghost. I handed the phone to my father.

"So this is…"

"Liam O'Reilly," I supplied.

"A handsome young man."

"Oh, yeah." For a too brief moment, my depression lifted.

"What are you going to do now?"

"What do you mean?" With a last look at Liam, I slipped the phone back into my purse.

"You're still planning on going to Virginia Tech this fall, aren't you?"

"Yeah." But it was months away. The summer loomed long and lonely.

"Have you given any thought to writing down your adventures?" The lounge chair squeaked under him as he shifted.

"Like a book?"

"Yes, like a book."

"Actually, I have. But not to sell. Just for myself, and for Aileen and Ethel, you know?"

"Self-publish then."

"I could, couldn't I?" I straightened, the seed planted. This was something I could do to honor Liam. I'd put everything down on paper so I'd never forget. I'd put the pictures in too.

"It's a story I'd love to read."

"I appreciate your interest. Thanks, Dad, for everything." I heaved to my feet.

"Hungry?" Dad asked.

"Starved." To my surprise, I realized it was true. My stomach gurgled at the image of Vel's fried chicken. I hesitated. "After all the drama, I'd rather not go back to the brunch."

"Marcy brought you back a plate." He threw his arm around me, and we walked companionably to the cottage, my head resting on his shoulder.

"I'm going to write a book, Marcy," I announced as we strolled into the kitchen. "And tell Liam's story."

"I'm sure it will be a bestseller," she said and poured me a glass of sweet tea. The cubes clinked as she handed it to me.

"Not that kind of book. I'm just going to have a few copies made." I took the glass and glugged thirstily.

"I'm going home, honey. Call if you need me. Why not stop by this week for dinner?" Dad patted me on the shoulder.

"I will." Guilt washed over me. I should have gone before.

He kissed me on the cheek and walked out.

"Are you better?" Marcy's gaze swept over my face, searching.

"It hurts." I rubbed my chest. "But people don't die of a broken heart." It made my jaws ache, but I managed to plaster a smile on my face.

I continued, determined, "I have you and the family. I'll write Liam's story. We'll go to school in the fall. I'll be fine."

Marcy opened her mouth. Before she could respond, the phone rang.

"I'll get it." She touched my arm, then headed for the phone.

I sank down into a kitchen chair, glad I no longer had to smile. I made wet intertwining circles on the table with the bottom of my glass as I rotated it back and forth.

Marcy popped her head back in. "It's Clayton."

I rolled my eyes. "I really don't…"

She threw up her hands. "You know how he can be. Short of hanging up on him, there was no putting him off."

"I've got no problem with you hanging up on him," I grumbled. "All right. All right." I pushed my chair away from the table and trudged to the phone. "Hello, Clayton."

"Hey, babe, what're you doing?"

Babe? "What do you want?" I sank down onto the sofa. I didn't have the energy to stand.

"I thought we'd take in a movie tonight. We haven't gone out in a while."

"I'm not in the mood for a movie." The abstract on the far wall done in shades of dark blue, black, and gray reflected my mood to a T.

"How about dinner then?"

"I don't think so."

"Come on, you have to eat," he coaxed.

"I'm in the middle of something." Or soon would be. I wanted to start my book. I needed a connection to Liam, no matter how tenuous.

"What?"

"I'm writing a book."

"Really?" Polite indifference came through the phone. Then his voice brightened. "That might be a nice little hobby for you after we marry."

"Excuse me?" That got my attention. I pulled the phone away from my ear and stared at it before continuing. "Are you insane?"

"Oh not right away." He went on to outline his plan, ignoring my last statement. "After I get my four-year degree, I'll be going on to grad school and I need to get established, but in a few years."

Marcy walked by, sipping on a can of soda. "Pull the plug," she advised in passing and kept going.

Good advice. I rubbed my head and closed my eyes. I didn't want to deal with this. The problem was I never wanted to deal with it. I took a deep breath. "Clayton, I don't think we should see each other anymore."

"What?" The voice on the other end of the phone sounded incredulous. Clayton Bradford III wasn't used to being dumped.

"We're through." There I'd said it. *Finally*. Relief washed through me…for about a nanosecond.

"You're tired. We'll talk about it tomorrow."

"What part of 'it's over' don't you understand?" I spoke slowly and carefully. Maybe he had a hearing problem I wasn't aware of. Elbow propped on the side of the couch, I held my head. The headache I'd kept at bay came thundering to the fore.

"Is it the wrong time of the month?"

"I can't believe you just said that. Goodbye, Clayton." I ended the call.

"Well, I did it, Liam. You never approved of him anyway, did you?" I spoke to the room at large.

There was no response. I hadn't expected any, but I'd hoped.

Marcy came back into the room and plopped down beside me. "Did you break it off?"

"There was nothing to break off. We were never an item. But yes, I did." I rubbed at the hollow spot under my left breastbone.

"You've had quite a time of it, haven't you?" Marcy said.

"Yeah, but I'll survive. I miss him."

"Goes without saying."

The doorbell rang.

"I'll get it." Marcy hopped off the couch.

"If it's Clayton, don't let him in."

"What about Patrick?"

I shook my head. "I just can't deal with another man right now."

"Gotcha." Marcy headed out of the room. She was gone for several minutes. She stepped back in wearing a curious little smile. "I know what you said, but I'll take care of this one if you're giving them up for a while."

"What are you talking about?" The comment confused me.

She held up a finger, walked out, and came back moments later with a nice-looking young man in tow, her hand on his arm.

I frowned. He looked vaguely familiar.

"Hello, Ms. King."

"Officer Atwell?" He didn't have on his blues or I would have recognized him immediately. He wore faded jeans and a button-up, short-sleeved, white shirt that set off an impressive set of pecs.

"I suppose 'I just happened to be in the neighborhood' is a bit lame?" He stuck his hands in his pockets, rocked on his heels, and grinned sheepishly.

"A bit."

"Cuz has a headache, but I for one am thrilled you stopped by, Officer Atwell."

"Please, call me Ryan."

"Ryan." Marcy looked into his eyes, fluttered her lashes, and stepped closer.

Ryan looked bedazzled. He cleared his throat. "That's quite a security system you've got."

Marcy and I looked blankly at each other.

"Thank you," Marcy said.

"Who lives in the mansion next door?" was Ryan's next conversational gambit.

Marcy made a dismissive gesture with her hand. "My parents. This is the guest cottage."

"The guest cottage?" His eyebrows rose.

I swallowed a giggle. If I wasn't so miserable, I'd be enjoying myself.

"Would you like me to show you around?" Marcy leaned against his arm and gave him her killer smile.

Ryan smiled back. I could have sworn he started to accept before he looked at me questioningly.

"Go right ahead. You're in good hands." I waved them on.

They walked out chatting.

Well, well, well, Marcy and the policeman. Wouldn't that be interesting? I certainly didn't know Ryan well, but what little I did know I liked. I approved of him for my cousin. And since I couldn't face any type of relationship, it simplified my life.

I pushed off the couch and headed to my bedroom. Without Marcy and Ryan around, silence closed in on me. It was hard to catch my breath, hard to move one foot in front of the other. I made it to my room and fell face down onto the bed. Depression enveloped me like a shroud. I would work on Liam's story later. Social interaction had held pain at bay. Now it flooded my system. I closed my eyes, and with no effort at all slid into oblivion.

* * * *

"Caitlin, wake up." Marcy shook my shoulder.

"Go away. I've barely closed my eyes."

"Caitlin, you've been out for five hours. Patrick's on the phone."

"Why do you keep making me take phone calls?" I mumbled and put the pillow over my head. "I'll call him later."

"This isn't healthy. Talk to Patrick." She plucked the pillow off my head.

"Give me a break." I grabbed the pillow away from her and stuck it back over my head.

"Ignoring everyone isn't going to help anything." She grabbed it back.

"Give me some grieving time."

"I gave you as much as you're going to get." Her arms hugged the pillow so I couldn't grab it back.

"A few measly days, get serious." I sat up.

"Just talk to Patrick, okay?"

"Sure." I pulled myself out of bed and trudged to the living room. Why hadn't he used my cell? I could have ignored that. Then again, he probably had.

"Patrick." I picked up the phone, slumped onto the couch, and let my head fall against the back cushion.

"Cat, how are you?"

Great. Peachy. How the heck do you think I am? I fell in love with a ghost and he left me. "What do you want, Patrick?"

"I've been worried about you. I wanted to make sure you were all right."

Concern came through in the warm timbre of his voice. The tight kernel of pain loosened, but it didn't go away. I doubted if it ever completely would, but there was something about Patrick that always made me feel better. "I appreciate that."

"How about if I pick up a couple of lattes and come over?"

I hesitated. "Patrick—"

Before I could refuse, he cut in, "I'll pick one up for Marcy too. What would she like?"

I didn't have the energy to argue. "Iced peppermint for both of us."

"I'm on my way."

"Okay." Boneless, I sunk deeper into the sofa.

"And, Cat?"

"Yes?"

"I won't overstay my welcome. I just want to see you."

"I know. Bye."

"Bye." As I hung up, Marcy appeared.

"Lurking?"

"Unashamedly listening." She laughed and sat down.

"Patrick's bringing us lattes." I pulled my legs under me and leaned my elbow on the arm of the sofa.

"He's a thoughtful man. You could do a lot worse."

"Give it a rest. Liam is barely gone."

"But he is gone."

"That one I've figured out for myself."

"Have you? There's not some part of you waiting for him to reappear in human form?" She watched me, her gaze searching.

"He's moved into the light." My heart tightened. I was happy for him, of course. But that didn't make being left behind any easier. "You seemed mighty interested in Ryan."

A flush traveled up her neck and added a nice rosy glow to her high cheekbones. "Your policeman is easy on the eyes and a decent guy." She tapped her lip and added thoughtfully. "Both he and Patrick are different from most of the men in our crowd."

"Yes, they are. And he's not my policeman."

"Do you have any interest in that direction?" She bit her lips together and watched me.

"Not even a little."

"Then you don't mind if I have a go at him?"

"Not in the least."

"Whew. That's a relief." She shook her head. "I don't know what it is about him, but I find him extremely appealing."

"You should see him in uniform." I grinned.

"I intend to." Her lips quirked upward.

Before I could respond, the doorbell rang.

"I'll get it." Marcy hopped up and trotted out of the room, her long legs moving at a brisk pace.

A moment later, Patrick came in carrying two lattes.

He handed me one. "That was fast." I looked over his shoulder. "Where's Marcy?"

"She mentioned painting her nails and disappeared." He eased down beside me and set his latte on the end table. With a touch as delicate as a surgeon's, he lifted my chin and studied me. "Even the circles under your eyes are lovely, more violet than black or gray. You're such a pretty thing."

Embarrassed, I jerked my head away. He let his hand fall to his side. "Can you talk about it?"

I didn't want to bring him pain, but I didn't want to lie to him either. In the long run, I had to believe the truth would hurt less. Besides, how vested could he be? We didn't know each other that well.

I lifted my chin and looked him straight in the eye. "I fell in love with a ghost."

"I got that part of it." He grimaced. "It's the rest I don't understand." "The rest?"

"You know, girl meets ghost, ghost sweeps her off her feet." His voice was light but his neck stiff. Cords stood out in his forearms.

"You won't believe this."

"Try me."

"My cousin purchased him on eBay."

"You're right. I don't believe it."

"Told ya."

"Even if I don't believe it, it sounds like a good story. Tell me." He leaned back into the cushions.

Silence thrummed between us. He watched me patiently.

"You win."

I pretended I didn't hear him murmur, "I doubt it."

The story came tumbling out. At times, he laughed appreciatively. At others, he shook his head in disbelief. When I'd finally finished, I leaned back against the cushions, my insides lighter, like some of the coiled tension had loosened.

"That's quite a story."

"It is, isn't it?" I picked up my latte. By now it was a bit watered down, but it didn't matter. "Thank you."

"No big. Even a poor college student can afford an occasional latte."

I shook my head and returned his smile. "That too. But mainly just for being. You seem to know exactly what I need even when I don't."

"It's a gift." He leaned over and kissed me lightly on the tip of my nose. "How about we watch some old movies? I brought some with me."

"I'm just not very good company tonight, maybe another time." I shifted and rubbed my arms. I was cold, always cold.

"Okay, not in the mood for movies. I get it." He pushed off the couch and looked down at me.

"I'm sorry."

"For what? I've got a backup plan." He hauled me to my feet and pulled me across the room.

"What are you doing?"

His fingers locked around mine, he led me through the door.

I tugged at his hand as he headed for his car. "I'm not going anywhere."

"Not a problem," he responded, his voice amicable. He stopped and looked around. "How deep is this lot?"

"About seven acres, I think," I answered, confused.

"That should work." He dropped my hand, opened the back seat of his car, and leaned in. "Any open spaces?"

"Yeah, out back." My interest came sluggishly to life.

He backed out of the car carrying a tripod and a telescope. "Let's star gaze."

"You came prepared for all contingencies, didn't you?" I said, unsure whether to be upset or touched.

"Yup, lead the way." He got a better grip on his equipment and turned toward me.

"Okay." Defeated, I walked around the hedges to my aunt and uncle's property behind the manse. We strolled in silence for a bit through gardens that smelled like sweet nectar. An occasional night bloomer's silvery head waved as a light breeze rustled through branches. Overhead a night bird twittered.

"Nice." Patrick's voice was quiet. The still night had that affect.

The path we were on led out of the garden to a wide open space, with a couple of old oaks breaking the stretch of flat green.

"This should do it." He looked around and stopped. With practiced ease, he settled the tripod and telescope. He slouched over, his eye on the eyepiece, his hiney, covered in baggy jeans, in the air. He pointed the scope toward the sky, made some adjustments, and grunted. "Take a look." He stepped back.

I put my eye to the scope. "Everything's blurry."

He made some quick adjustments, turning the circular cylinder first left, then right. "How about now?"

The stars sprang into view. The sky came alive like a thousand sparkling diamonds. "Oh, Li—"

I stopped myself from saying, *Liam you should see this.* In such a short time, he'd become an integral part of my life. We'd bonded, become one person, at least in the metaphysical sense. Instead, my eyes filled with tears and my heart murmured, *Are you up there, Liam? Are you happy?*

As if in response, one lone star shot across the sky toward me, then disappeared. The stars blurred as my eyes filled.

"Thank you, Patrick. That was truly wonderful." My throat was thick and tears rolled down my cheeks.

"Then why are you crying?" He stepped closer and thumbed a tear off my face, then another. "Don't cry, pretty girl, please don't cry." He slid a warm comforting arm around me, leaned down, and kissed one wet cheek, then the other. His lips hovered near mine. I knew what was coming. I didn't try to stop him. Liam was gone. Patrick was here. His lips met mine, tentative and warm. His grip tightened.

My throat swelled shut. I couldn't breathe. This wasn't right. I shoved against him, panting. "I'm sorry. I just can't."

His arms dropped to his side. "Too soon. I knew that. But for a moment it felt like..." His voice trailed off.

"Yeah, I know. But I just can't."

"It's okay. No rush. We've got all the time in the world. Maybe we should call it a night."

I nodded, unable to speak.

"Will you be all right? I could always stay over. Sleep on the couch." He lifted my chin, his gaze searching mine.

"Thank you. I'm truly touched. I'll be all right. Marcy's in the house. It's time I got some of this down on paper. It will help me heal."

"And hopefully give you closure." He gave me a rueful grin.

"Patrick, I..."

He interrupted me. "I know this may not work out the way I want it to." His gaze held mine. "You're worth the risk."

Was I? I wondered. Since I'd met Liam and Patrick, my former dating values seemed rather shallow.

"Well, I guess I'd better get going." He picked up his equipment and tucked it under his arm. With his free hand, he clasped mine and we walked to his car.

He shoved the telescope into the back seat and leaned against the door. "I'll call you."

"Okay." With any other guy, I'd wonder if he meant it after the fiasco in the backyard, but Patrick wouldn't have said it if he didn't mean it. I hoped I wasn't setting him up.

He shoved away from the car, took my hand, kissed my palm, and closed my fingers around it. "Get some sleep, sweet Cat."

His gentleness undid me. My eyes pricked again. "Thanks." I waited till he drove off before I trudged back in the house. Once in the bedroom, I dropped across the bed, exhausted, waiting for sleep to overtake me.

It never came. A thousand pictures of Liam swirled through my mind: Liam stretched out by the pool, accompanying me on my dates with Patrick, the look on his face as he rode in Marcy's Vette, and finally the shooting star.

Uttering a word my mom wouldn't have approved of, I flung myself out of bed and headed for my tiny study. I turned on the light and stood there. Could I do this?

I slid into the chair and pulled up a blank document. I looked at it for a long time, my mind racing. Finally, I began.

Liam O'Reilly grew up in the little town of Ruby Falls. He came to manhood during the tumultuous times of the Civil War. But war wasn't what killed him.

Chapter 18

The August sun beat down with merciless intensity, humidity so thick you could cut it with a knife. The family and Patrick stood grouped around Marcy's Vette and my bug, Pinkie, both cars packed so tightly there was barely room for the drivers.

"Honey, don't you want us to help you move in?" It was Mom's swan song. She'd been singing it monotonously ever since I told her I wanted to move in by myself with no parental help. She dabbed at a bead of perspiration on her forehead with a tissue.

"You were there just last week and Parents' Weekend is coming up in two weeks. I'll see you then." I also knew my lines by heart. Aunt Janet and Uncle Leon came over and gave me a brief hug and kiss before they moved to do the same with their daughter.

Mom sighed, tearing up, and hugged me. "Call me the minute you get there."

"I will. Love you."

"Love you, baby." She gave me another fierce hug, then stepped back as Dad took her place. He slipped me a slim brown package.

"You got it back already?" I'd spent six weeks writing Liam's story. I'd locked myself in my study only coming out to eat and sleep. When it was finished, I'd given it to Dad to proof. He'd read it, put his seal of approval on it, and offered to get it printed.

My fingers slid over the hardbound book. "It feels awfully thin for three copies."

"This one's yours. I went ahead and sent the other two to Ms. Aileen and Ms. Ethel."

"Thanks, Dad. And they're the only copies you had made?"

He crossed his heart. "The only copies. I know how personal this is to you, and I respect that. If you choose to pursue it, you've got the makings of a damn fine reporter. And you've got the skill."

"Thanks." Pleasure flooded my system. Coming from my father, it was no small praise. He drew me to him, held me a moment, kissed my forehead, then let go. "Figure out how to be happy, Caitlin."

"I'm happy."

He looked at me, his gaze profoundly sad. I'd always been able to fib to Mom, but Dad saw right through me.

"I'll try," I amended.

"Once you're in school, you'll be too busy to brood."

"I don't brood."

He lifted his eyebrows.

"Well maybe a little."

"I better let Patrick say good-bye." He smiled and stepped back. Patrick had spent a lot of time with me over the summer. He and Dad had hit it off.

I straightened my shoulders. There was something I had to do, and I wasn't looking forward to it.

"When are you heading back?" I asked Patrick, clutching my book in my right hand.

"Tomorrow." He rocked back on his heels, his hands shoved in his pockets. "I'll call you."

"Patrick..." I shifted my glance to my relatives, who'd moved discreetly away.

"Don't say it, Cat." His voice, like mine, was pitched low.

"I'm not a good bet. I know my timing stinks, but I don't see myself being ready to be involved with anyone for a long time."

I'd tossed and turned all night, trying to figure out what to do. Patrick had been my lifeline over the summer. Without him, life would have been difficult indeed. But he deserved so much more than what I could give him. "I want you to date other people. The best I can ever offer you is friendship." I forced the words out. It was the right thing to do even if it didn't feel like it.

He winced. I could see his hands fist in his pockets. Before he could respond, I took a small step toward him. "I can never repay everything you've done for me. You managed to glue some of the broken pieces back together. The best thing I can do for you is cut you loose." It hurt to say it. God, it hurt. I'd become way too dependent on him. I reached out and touched his cheek. "We'll always be the best of friends."

"The ole 'let's be friends routine,' hey?"

I cringed.

His gaze shifted to the ground, then settled on my face. "It's okay. I knew the score when I got into this. I know I'll always come in second to your ghost, but I'm willing to settle."

I shook my head. "No. Don't even think about settling. You deserve so much more. I wish I could be the person you need, but I'm still broken." My voice caught. My eyes filled.

He grabbed me and held me close. "I'll be waiting if you change your mind," he whispered in my hair.

I almost did. It would be so easy to settle, to have someone love me and take care of me, even if I didn't return his feelings. So easy. But I'd meant it. He deserved more. I couldn't be selfish any longer. I took a deep breath. "I'll always be your number one fan," I said with a shaky smile.

He kissed my cheek. "Be happy."

I wished people would stop saying that.

"You too," I whispered, my throat clogged, my eyes burning. "I'll see you at school."

"See you around." He turned on his heel and strode to his car.

I opened my car door and paused. My dad stood with his arm around my mom. Uncle Leon and Aunt Janet held hands. I wondered if they'd figured out why Patrick had left. By the look on my dad's face, at least he had.

Marcy gave an impatient toot of her horn. I slid into the car and started the motor. Before I pulled out, I tore off the brown paper. A small hardback with a solid black cover and gold lettering said Liam O'Reilly.

"Thank you, Dad," I whispered. I started the motor and backed up my bug as Marcy rolled onto the street. With a wave to the family, she took off.

I bit my lip, waved good-bye, and followed her. I stole one last look in the rearview mirror. Sitting in the driver's seat of his car, Patrick raised a hand in farewell.

* * * *

It was our fourth week on campus.

Marcy and I shared a dorm room. I spent a lot of time at the library, and occasionally dragged her with me when she wasn't with her sorority sisters or going to a frat party. It was where we were headed now.

It had been a bad day. I hadn't aced an Econ test. I'd been too edgy, couldn't focus. But worst of all, I'd smelled cinnamon and limes. Not the intense scent Liam gave off, just a faint, occasional whiff. I knew it was my imagination, but it had driven me crazy. Still was.

"Caitlin."

"Hmm?"

"I've asked you the same question three times. What's wrong?" Marcy queried as we pushed through the wide doors of the library.

"Nothing. I'm fine," I forced out. I couldn't burden my cousin with my anxiety. Marcy was worried enough about me.

She didn't contradict me, just reached out with her free hand and gave me a hug. "Of course you are. Have you heard from Patrick lately?"

I wasn't sure the subject change was an improvement, but I went along gamely. "Yeah. There's a little redhead after him. I wish her luck. He deserves someone that's head over heels for him."

"Yeah."

We fell silent for a moment before Marcy asked, "Did I tell you Ryan threw Clayton out of the house this summer?"

I stopped in my tracks. "What?"

She nudged me forward and giggled. "I'd told Ryan about Clayton, so when he showed up, Ryan told him he'd have you file stalking charges against him and throw him in jail, if he came near you again."

"Way to go, Ryan. That must be why he only calls and stopped coming over. I can't figure out what part of 'we're through' he doesn't understand."

"The boy is certainly self-absorbed," she agreed.

"You've got that right. You better hold on to Ryan. He's a keeper."

"I'm thinking seriously about it."

The soles of our shoes echoed against the marble tile as we continued down the hall. We stepped into a large room filled with tables. "Where shall we study?" I whispered.

She pointed at an open table farther back and to our right. "How about that one?"

"Okay."

As we walked, I sniffed cautiously. The only smell was old books, perfume, and aftershave.

"Perfect," Marcy said as we tossed down our books, pulled out our laptops, and plugged them in. I was working on an English paper that wasn't due for two weeks. Marcy had a paper due in Sociology the next day.

Soon, I was engrossed in the world of Mary Shelley.

"My God, if that isn't the most gorgeous man I've ever seen," she breathed in my ear. I ignored her and kept typing. Marcy was ambidextrous when she studied. She could work, flirt, and chatter all at the same time. For the most part, I tuned her out.

"He looks like…" Her voice trailed off. She pushed to her feet, chair scraping against the floor. "Caitlin," she whispered.

"Hmm." I didn't take my eyes off the keyboard as I tried, in the most concise manner possible, to explain why Frankenstein was such a classic.

The smooth waterfall voice hit me before the words. "Good evening, Marcy."

I froze.

Marcy stuttered, an unusual occurrence for my outgoing cousin. "Do we know each other?"

"I'm your former roommate. Or should I say Caitlin's ghost?"

My hands fell away from the keyboard. The blood drained from my face and my ears buzzed. With a stiff, jerky motion, I lifted my head, my breath lodged in my throat.

Liam smiled at me, his heart in his eyes. At least, I assumed it was Liam. He wore a black polo and faded jeans. His wonderful head of hair was cropped much closer to his head than I was used to seeing. Trembling, I reached out to him, expecting to feel a tingle of electricity as my fingers grasped air. Instead, I touched warm flesh.

My throat constricted and my eyes stung.

He held out his hand. I clasped it and reveled in the unbelievable heat and texture of it. "How?" was all I could manage.

He pulled me to my feet. "Let's take a walk and I'll explain."

Marcy sat down with a thump on the hard wood chair, for once at a loss for words.

"I'll see your cousin home. Would you bring her books and laptop?"

She nodded, still speechless. Me too, for that matter.

When we walked out of the building, the warm night air hit me. Moths did their death dance around outdoor lights shining down on the sidewalk. Liam led me to a stone seat and drew me down.

He still smelled of cinnamon and limes. "How?" It seemed to be the only thing I was capable of saying.

"Darned if I know." He laughed, a joyous sound. "It's pretty hazy and getting more so by the minute. But I'll try to explain.

"It was like I was in what you'd call a time continuum, like resting in this white space, aware of others in a shadowy kind of way, like me. As close as I can tell, it was a healing period for the spirit. Scents surrounded me: fresh air, honey, and sunshine. I floated in light and listened to the soft lazy lap of the seas." He gave a helpless shrug. "Time had no meaning.

Gradually, all the pain from the war, my sister's death, being locked in that black void for so long, it went away.

"It was at that point I became aware of a greater being. I never saw her, but I felt such warmth and love." He gave me a shy smile. "It's like I feel when I'm with you. This presence, for lack of a better term, spoke to me without using words, just imparted the thoughts. She told me I was ready to move on, that it was time.

"I could move into the light forever with Anna, William, and Ezra or I could come back and be with the one I loved." He raised his hand palm up and shook his head as if unable to put into words his experience. "Like reincarnating. The best way I can describe it is you get a second chance if you've left things undone on earth.

"Well that was a no brainer, as you'd say." He chuckled. "The next thing I know, I'm plopped down here in the dead of night, naked as a jaybird."

I put my hand to my mouth to stifle a giggle at the mental image. "How did you get clothes?"

He cleared his throat. "I borrowed them."

My eyes widened. "You stole them? That is so un-Liam-like."

He lifted his chin. "I prefer the term borrowed. I'll make it up to the laddie. My options were limited."

"So you arrived with nothing? No social security card? No credit card? No clothes?"

"That's right, nothing but my bare skin."

"We're going to have to enlist Dad's help." I was getting excited. This was going to be fun. Liam would have to have a whole new persona created. And I was just the girl to help him do it. Another thought hit me. "How did you find me?"

"Oh, that was easy enough. Think of me as a compass and you the magnet. You're my heart, Caitlin." He lifted my hand and kissed it. My stomach fluttered and my pulse raced. No wonder I loved this man. No one else had ever made me feel this way. No one else ever would.

He continued to hold my hand as he leaned toward me, his expression intense. "I want to be with you, Caitlin. Now. Forever."

My eyes filled. "I'm so glad," I whispered, my heart overflowing with happiness. I didn't care how or why, but the impossible had happened.

"There's been something I've wanted to do since the first moment I laid eyes on you." He dropped my hand, put his arms around me, and held me in a loose circle.

There it was. I'd missed that soft rolling accent that sounded like the sensuous slide of velvet when he spoke. I leaned into him, but he surprised me by clasping my arms and holding me away.

"Ye didn't go and get engaged to Patrick, did ye?" His voice sounded strained, his expression, even in shadows, looked anxious.

"No. Patrick is a wonderful man. But there's only one man for me, now or ever, Liam O'Reilly."

He drew me closer. "The poor sod. What about that arse of a Clayton, have you given him the heave ho?"

"No, but it's not from lack of trying. He can't seem to see past his own significance."

His eyes gleamed with anticipation. "He will when I tell him. Now where were we?" His lips hovered mere inches from mine. Warm hard arms drew me closer. "Caitlin," he breathed.

Impatient with the wait, I reached up, grabbed two handfuls of thick silky hair, and pulled his head down. Our lips met and our tongues collided. Thunder rolled. Streaky flashes of lightning that had nothing to do with malignant spirits speared behind my eyelids. Months of pain and listlessness dissipated like smoke.

"Welcome to the twenty-first century, Liam O'Reilly," I murmured when we finally drew apart.

"It's going to take some getting used to. The lasses are more forward than in my day." His eyes glinted as he smiled at me with that crooked grin that always left me weak in the knees.

"You have no idea." I tugged his head back down to show him exactly what he could expect.

"I'll try to bear up somehow," he whispered against my mouth before his lips closed on mine.

My head whirled in a dizzy spiral of pleasure. I shifted closer and moved my hands to his shoulders to get a better grip. My flesh and blood ghost cooperated with enthusiasm. I had no doubt he'd manage the transition just fine. Then all thought fled as I lost myself in the wonder of him. Finally, I was home… And so was he.

Meet the Author

Sandra Cox writes Young Adult Fantasy, Paranormal and Historical Romance, and Metaphysical non-fiction. She lives in sunny North Carolina with her husband, a brood of critters, and an occasional foster cat. Although shopping is high on the list, her greatest pleasure is sitting on her screened-in porch, listening to the birds, sipping coffee and enjoying a good book. She's a vegetarian and a Muay Thai enthusiast. Please visit Sandra's blog at sandracox.blogspot.com, find her on Facebook, or follow her on twitter.com@Sandra_Cox

LOVE, LATTES AND MUTANTS

Finding love is hard, even when you aren't a mutant.

Like most seventeen-year-olds, Piper Dunn wants to blend in with the crowd. Having a blowhole is a definite handicap. A product of a lab-engineered mother with dolphin DNA, Piper spends her school days hiding her brilliant ocean-colored eyes and sea siren voice behind baggy clothing and ugly glasses. When Tyler, the new boy in school, zeroes in on her, ignoring every other girl vying for his attention, no one, including Piper, understands why...

Then Piper is captured on one of her secret missions rescuing endangered sea creatures and ends up in the same test center where her mother was engineered. There she discovers she isn't the only one of her kind. Joel is someone she doesn't have to hide from, and she finds herself drawn to the dolph-boy who shares her secrets. Talking to him is almost as easy as escaping from the lab. Deciding which boy has captured her heart is another story...

A Lyrical e-book on sale now.

Chapter 1

"Miss Dunn, are we keeping you awake?" Mr. Grumble's sarcastic remark draws titters from the class.

I jerk upright. "No, Mr. Grumble." Heat floods my face.

"Glad to hear it." He turns back to the whiteboard and writes an equation with a red marker.

I slink down in my seat and push my tinted glasses back up on my nose.

The class's attention shifts from my discomfort. Some to the board where Mr. Grumble is still writing the equation, some to flirt outrageously with the new boy in class, some to sneak out their phones and send a text, which most definitely isn't allowed.

Only the new girl—she and the boy are twins—takes time to give me a commiserating smile. I grimace back.

She's always polite and kind in her dealings with me, something that confuses me.

Now her brother, Tyler, although polite, is oblivious. Comes from having girls trip all over him I guess.

The bell rings. I pick up my books. When the room clears, I slide out of my seat. Holly, the new girl, is waiting for me, her entourage grouped around her. She smiles. I glance over my shoulder but the warm smile is for me. She waves her friends on. "I'll catch up."

They move forward like a herd of sheep, perplexed expressions on their faces. Can't blame them, I'm perplexed myself. I don't get a lot of attention. My blonde hair is scraped back into a ponytail and pinned in a wrap-up sponge barrette. My clothes are baggier than a rapper's and as unassuming as I can find. In other words, the total package is boring. I wouldn't go so far as to say that's the way I like it, but it's necessary.

"Hi." Holly shifts her books to her other arm.

"Hi." I clutch my book bag to my chest, not making eye contact.

She falls in step beside me. "Bad luck hitting Grumble's radar. Half the kids in class sleep through his lectures."

I shrug.

"Would you like to grab a latte after school?" is her next conversational gambit.

"Why?" No doubt, I sound like a total jerk, but there's no point in encouraging a friendship. Though the idea of an icy latte and girl talk appeals. A lot. If the situation were different, I'd be a girlie-girl, but it's not and I'm not.

Chatter surrounds us. Juniors and seniors hurry down the hall to their classes. Rosemont is built like a letter U. Freshmen and sophomores on one side, juniors and seniors on the other; the gym and stage merge in the center.

"Because you look like you can use a friend. I know I can."

"I have friends. Everyone has friends." Okay, they're people and creatures I've saved and they don't know who I am, but I'm sure I could count on them in a pinch.

"And a sense of humor." Holly laughs. "Who'd a thought?" She looks me over. Her lips twitch; she tries to hold back a smile.

I grin reluctantly. Then what she tacked on sinks in. "You're the most popular girl in school right now. Why would you possibly need a friend?"

She bites her lips and looks at me.

I cave. "Okay, as a matter of fact, I'd love a latte, but I warn you I'm not noted for my sterling conversation. I'm clueless about the latest trends in hair, clothes, or shoes."

At that moment, her hottie-of-a-brother Tyler lopes by. "Hol," he acknowledges his shorter, fraternal twin. He gives me an absent nod. Not unkind, worse, indifferent. I'm damn sick of fading into the woodwork.

She looks at me as if she's waiting for me to figure it out. I glance from her to her brother. Right. Holly's pretty but hardly drop-dead gorgeous. Though her vivacity makes up for it. And she is the new kid. Still, I get it. The girls are sucking up in the hopes of scoring with her brother.

"Alright, I'll meet you at the Pink Cat Coffee Shop at four o'clock."

She smiles and her pretty features light up. It takes her out of the attractive—but not mega hot—category and puts her in her brother's. "See you at the Pink Cat. Don't stand me up."

"Hey, it's not a date you know." I'm a firm believer in gay rights, but it's so not my thing.

She giggles. "My heart belongs to Ben Henley." She names the football player who was firmly ensconced as the most popular boy at Rosemont until her twin arrived on the scene.

"I'll be there," I promise and head for social studies.

It may not have been smart but having a normal teenage destination to look forward to will certainly make the rest of the day easier to get through. I lied when I said I wasn't interested in hairstyles and shoes. I love girlie stuff. Anyone with a drop of girl DNA loves shoes.

I look at my clothes and sigh. I'll be so glad to get home where I can shuck them like a used cocoon.

For now, I continue the role of uninteresting, blah nerd. I do such a good job even the geeks keep their distance.

With a sigh, I thump my books on my desk and slide into my seat.

For the next forty minutes, I immerse myself in the effects of mob behavior on normal people. As soon as the bell rings, I shoot out of my seat and head for the door.

I hit the hall at a fast pace, not paying as much attention as I should and collide with Edgar the Asshole Fahrenbacher, the most egotistical senior in Rosemont. Although, why anyone with a name like Edgar should be arrogant is beyond me. Maybe he's overcompensating. He calls himself the Stallion. With chestnut hair, tight jeans, and a swagger, he's not bad looking, but his looks don't match his ego.

"Oof." My books go flying and so do his. They hit the floor with a thud.

"Sorry," I mumble, head down, heat shooting through my cheeks.

"Not only are you a mouse, you're a klutz. Pick my books up." Totally humiliated, I bend to comply, hating every minute of it. I would much rather knock him on his swaggering butt and I could do it, too, if I weren't trying to keep a low profile. Well, I could in the water anyway. I can hold my own against anybody in the water.

When I reach for his chemistry book, he kicks it farther down the hall. Embarrassment turns to mad. What a total jerk. Before I totally blow my cover, hands reach out and sweep up the books.

"Which ones are yours?"

I look into piercing blue eyes and forget to breathe—and everything else for that matter.

"Which are yours?" Holly's brother repeats patiently.

Mutely, I point at the top three. He hands them to me before he helps me to my feet. The rest he thrusts at Edgar. "I'm sure you can get the other book yourself," he says easily to Edgar.

Edgar nods, scowling at the interruption of his version of pull-the-wings-off-the-fly.

"Thank you." Breathless, lost in the depths of those deep pools of blue, I forget to disguise my voice. Fortunately—or unfortunately in this case—it doesn't go with my nerd image. Gramps compares it to mermaids' and sirens' songs. For an old guy, he's a romantic. So when I talk, I try to drop toward an unobtrusive alto.

Tyler's head jerks up. He wasn't paying attention to who he was helping, just being kind to one of the lesser beings. For the first time, he really looks at me and frowns, no doubt trying to equate the voice with the nerd.

I get a firm grip on my books and my raging hormones, and walk hastily away. I can feel his gaze boring into my back, probably trying to see past the shapeless clothes. I shudder, pick up my pace and, of course, trip. I keep a firm grip on my books, right myself, and keep going.

Fahrenbacher's hateful laughter rings in my ears. If only there was a convenient hole to crawl into. My sensitive hearing picks up a murmured, "What a voice."

Tyler's comment echoes in my head as I hurry through wide swinging doors escaping toward sunshine and a blue cloudless sky. I breathe in fresh air, yearning for the scent of salt water.

I turn right amid the cluster of excited voices around me—also anxious to escape the strictures of high school—and head for the coffee shop. It's only a block away. I'll come back later and pick up Beulah, my old truck.

When I arrive at the Pink Cat, Holly has already confiscated a booth. Of course, it's filled by a couple of the more popular girls in school. This is so not a good idea. She smiles and motions me over.

I shake my head and straighten my shoulders. I'll at least get my latte. I wait in line and, when I get to the counter, mumble my order.

Ignoring Holly, I grab my latte and head for the door.

"Piper," Holly's voice rings out. I cringe but take another determined step toward the door.

"Piper," Holly bellows again.

I sigh. So much for anonymity. I turn and prepare for twenty minutes of hell. After that, I'll make my escape. This is such a stupid idea.

I drag my feet over to her table.

"There you are." She beams. "Sit down. Piper's going to help me with my chemistry," she explains to the two cheerleaders sitting with her. They rise with alacrity.

"Uh, catch you later, Hol. Cheerleading practice starts in half an hour," the taller one says.

"Give our best to your brother," the other chimes in.

"Of course," Holly responds sweetly.

They grab their drinks, murmur a hello in my direction, and trot out the door.

"You were going to stand me up," she accuses.

I shrug. "I'm lousy at chemistry."

"I'm pretty good at it," she responds with a mischievous smile.

"You're bad. I like it." As always, except for that one slip with her brother, I use my nerd voice. This girl is way too bright.

She gives a modest smile and sips her cappuccino, loaded with whipped cream and chocolate sprinkles.

She glances disparagingly at my no-frills iced latte. "That looks very plain."

"It fits me." I take a sip and sigh with pleasure as the bite of espresso and the smooth taste of chocolate coalesce and slide down my throat.

She leans forward, her expression both curious and knowing. "Plain's exactly what you're not, but for some reason you want people to think you are."

Startled, I jerk upright. The cup, slick with condensation, starts to slip from my hands. I set it down hastily.

"What are you talking about?" My stomach jumps.

"You're the only girl in school who hasn't tried to befriend me in order to get to my brother. It piqued my curiosity." She places her elbows on the table, rests chin in hands, and studies me.

I squirm. "He's not my type. I've barely noticed him."

"Oh, you've noticed him all right. Even with those tinted glasses, I've seen you follow his progress down the hall. So why haven't you tried to worm your way into my good graces?"

Why indeed? My brain shuts down. "I'm shy," is all I can think of.

"Maybe." She sips her frothy drink and leans back, her gaze still on me.

"Your brother isn't the complete God's gift to women everyone seems to think he is." Liar. Liar.

"That's telling me," an amused voice speaks over my shoulder.

Crap! Busted.